Other books by Noy Holland

The Spectacle of the Body

What Begins with Bird

Swim for the Little One First

Bird

a novel

---

noy holland

COUNTERPOINT
BERKELEY

Library of Congress Cataloging-in-Publication Data

Holland, Noy, 1960-
 Bird : a novel / Noy Holland.
     pages ; cm
 ISBN 978-1-61902-564-6 (hardcover)
 1. Married women—Fiction. 2. Adultery—Fiction. 3. Domestic
fiction. I. Title.

 PS3558.O3486B57 2015
 813'.54—dc23

2015009412

Cover design by Kelly Winton
Interior design by Domini Dragoone

Counterpoint Press
2560 Ninth Street, Suite 318
Berkeley, CA 94710
www.counterpointpress.com

Printed in the United States of America
Distributed by Publishers Group West

10 9 8 7 6 5 4 3 2 1

FOR GORDON

He crossed her wrists behind her, walked her into the room. She was gowned in a towel from the tub, damp still, the day passing—cold, the green fuse blown. The city was flattened, looked to be; it was a poster of itself, grainy, famous in any light. He walked her where she could see it, where she could see the bridge, the man on a thread descending, his tiny pointed flame. She saw the hot blue bramble of welder's sparks fizzing out over the river. Across the river: the fabulous city.

He had set screw eyes in the floor. The floor was grooved, adrift with hair, the deep tarry blue of the ocean. He trained the heater on a patch of floor to warm the boards she would lie on. He pulled the towel off, helped her down in stages, onto her knees, her back.

The boards were gummy; they smelled of paint. They smelled of his dog who leaked in her sleep. She let him tie her—wrist and wrist and ankles. As he wished. He arranged her as he wished. He spread out her hair like a headdress, tall, like grass the wind has knocked down. He turned her toes out. He turned her wrists up when he tied her.

Something small—a bird—several—wobbled, blown behind her, the flock a scattering of ash in the wind in the cold above the river, the barges moored. The garbage scow. He lifted her head, knotted the scarf at the back of her head, the scarf snug across her eyes, her mother's scarf, across her mouth and nose. The scarf smelled of her mother. He trained the heater on her, and the cooling fan, oscillating, faint. He lit a candle, tipped it into the wind the fan made, and the wax blew hot, dispersing—sparkler, pod, nematocyst, a burn that lights and shrinks. He let the wax mound on the skin of her wrists—to mark the place, or seal it: here was the first place he touched her. Here was the mineral seep, the drip in a cave, the years passing. Here a notch—where the tendons of her neck knit into her chest and the wax would catch and pool. He said nothing. He scarcely touched her. Thrust into her once and walked out.

She heard him go. Two doors, the last stairs, hello on the stoop, he was gone.

A day a day: it passes. Gone: and not: and so again.

And so it passes. The last of the sun, a cooling wind. He was gone an hour, two, gone shopping. The only light in the room was the light of the street she could see through the scarf he had tied across her face and from the orange

2

glow of the heater, round, a fallen moon, its motor hum-ming. She heard rats plumping their nests in the walls and the creak of the beaten wings of birds falling out of the wind in the airshaft.

She waked, and knew by this that she had been sleep-ing. She had been flying her mother again on a ridge by a string like a kite. She could tell: she waked with her mother's same question.

Who will die when I die?

It was Mickey's question too.

She waked hungry. A baby cried, pushed down the street in a carriage. The wheels dropped into a crack in the street and the baby hiccupped.

"Whoops," said the mother.

It was too late to be out. It was too late to creep through the sumac with them and throw a stick in the river. Too long—this. Prank. She wanted up.

A siren set out. Bird tried to sing: the one about old Dixie, a favorite of her mother's, her mother newly dead, and Bird was alone in Brooklyn, and hot, and cold, and lashed to the floor by the man she loved and he was gone off from her and never coming home. She would starve here, freeze, she didn't know which. Mickey was dead or dying, drowned. He had been struck down, murdered, ferried to the ER, fer-ried to the morgue. The sirens passed, dimming, quit.

Such a boy. A boy who knew his knots.

She smelled soup. Men and women all over the country were sitting down to soup. Coming home. *Hello, mother.*

"Get your boots off," say the mothers, "get your coat."

Bird wanted to say it too. A little habit. She wanted to tell him to take his boots off twice a day for fifty years. She wanted to sort his socks for him and soak the spots from his clothes. She'd make biscuits. Swore it. And she would never use his comb. Bird would never use his toothbrush. She would always keep the sink clean. She would always ask first. She would leave a light on. She would not eat all the popcorn. She would leave his hats alone.

There he was. That was the key in the lock, the door-knob jammed into the divot it had made in the plaster of the entry wall. He left his boots on.

She married another. Mothered another.

Come here.

She heard him moving—the long stride, he wore his boot-heels down, moving among the—*ruins*, she wants to say, *rooms.* She said his name once and nobody answered.

It was not him. It wasn't like him.

Of course it was.

Her scalp fell away from her face; her brain dropped back in her head.

He brought her honey, the little bear warmed in his pocket. Lemon, he brought, and custard. Berries, aspara-gus, cream. He left the lights off, he took his time for a time. He meant to feed her first, he left the scarf on. "Guess. What's your hurry?"

He fed her lilac. He fed her persimmon—she had no idea—a food like refrigerated satin. Saltines. Marmalade and corn-fed beef and puffy milky biscuits. Frozen beer. Bedroom food. "Be still. Be still."

He would not be hurried. He turned the fan off. He turned the heater off. He wanted it quiet. He wanted them to hear. He slid his belt off, and swung the buckle across her mouth. "Say something," he whispered.

"Welcome home."

"You don't quit."

"Get this thing off," she said. "I want to see."

He pulled her scarf off. Mickey reached up and behind himself to bunch up his shirt at the collar.

It always took her, this simple act: the give in it, the show. How his chest broadened out, the wings went wide. The globe of muscle swelled out of his arm, glided away from his elbow: that. Simple act. A man undressing. Look. Look away. Any man is stronger than she is. Any freak on the street can take her—as he wishes, if he wishes. There is that. The fact of power; the fresh display.

And something more. He tugged his shirt up. He had to hang down his head to do it. He had to offer his neck, the hinge was open, the predator's handle of bone. Pretty, how he gave himself to it. His back softened, curved.

"Stop," she said. "I want to see."

He had his shirt across his face, he couldn't see. His arms were hung up, hanging down. He was wide open. She saw the shadowy scoop where his skull hooked in, a boy, just, tender, a girl dipping her hair in a stream. He would never be more lovely.

His face appeared. He looked down at her, his eyes near-white, boy-blue.

Something was wrong with him. He was weeping. The wind had torn up his hair.

"Mickey," she said. She called him Bird sometimes, his name for her, mistaken. "Mickey, you came home."

The day begins. Nothing will stop it.

The phone rings in the dark. Word finds its way along— no matter how far out you live, no matter what you say.

For years now, Bird has said it, for all the years since she has seen Mickey, all the things she has thought to say.

"I wish you'd stop," Bird says.

But this is Suzie. Newsy Suzie. Her voice high and bright. "It's me."

"Me too," Bird says. "I was sleeping. You have no fuck-ing clue."

What Suzie has is the next word on Mickey. She has a new name to give Bird. She has had the names down the years, a trade sometimes. Beatrice. Once a dancer, Brigitte, a girl who painted. Rosemarie. Country girls, exotics. Clara, Angelina, Racine.

"That's enough," Bird tells her.

"Oh it isn't. I keep you posted. Early girl news. He moved."

Moved, moved again. He thought to marry. He'd marry another, think of that, just as Bird had.

"He'll never marry," Suzie says, "he's like me. She would have to swear to die in three months' time of an incommunicable disease. I don't care who—Raquel, Ruby Lou, Victorine. He's like me."

Suzie lives among the samplings. The saplings, and the fathery men. Men and boys and girls. Ship to shore; hand to mouth; bed to bed. Not for her: the leaky tit, the pilly slipper. The dread of the phone that rings in the dark: *It's your turn next to suffer.*

"You hear nothing," Suzie claims, "you can't stand to, not a whiff of the world, a radio show. You cringe at the least of the news."

Which is true. And the rest of what Suzie says? This much is true, too—that the feeling is forever gone from Bird, god willing: of disappearing, of ever again being alone. Lonely doll.

"Remember," Suzie insists, "the sentence you get to finish? The dream you're not wrangled from?"

The next first kiss to fall into.

"The old looseness, come on, you must miss it. You miss it. Your brain makes a drug to subdue you is all. Look, I see it. Suzie sees it. Those babies are everywhere at you, needing anything they find. Your every living tissue, sugar, is pressed into service—gone."

Bird makes her slow laps as she listens—kitchen, woodstove, dripping milk, her shirtfront sopped, stewed in sour juices. She holds the phone out away from her ear: Suzie's on a tear. It's a club, Suzie claims, and she's not in it, thanks. No, no thank you, honest, she's not signing up to stew. Talky, stewy mother-club, virtuous, how little sleep and still she—look at her!—still she's cheerful. Seems to be, look at her, cheerful. Or maybe she's just smug, Suzie says. Clubby, you know, needed, every last speck of the day. Mama near. Little wife. A little respite comes, a little breath: nobody needs her! But she can't quite believe it, or let herself step outside.

"When's the last you stepped outside?" Suzie asks.

Or: "When'd you last look at your backside? That's the flapping you feel when you walk, sugar. You need to walk, sugar. You need to move."

He moved to France. Moved to pecan country.

Wise boy, getting out, flee the season. Winter coming on. *Oh I could help,* Bird thinks, at least she thought it then.

Pecan country. Pecans, best little nut. She could toss her smelly boots out, toss her stinking hat. Lie among the trees, among the shadows. She would like that. Watch the tough nuts fall.

She thinks of a boy in Kansas hung up on a swing, cripple boy, a boy they saw once, a little rope swing, a log on a rope, among the shadows. Among the signs. She and Mickey drove a Drive Away out, setting out from Brooklyn, dark, when the stars lined up how they sometimes do and anything you look at, everything's a sign. SLEEP SLEEP SLEEP, the sign says. It says, *Move while you still can.*

The dog was dead, the ragtop towed. The up-neighbors tub had fallen through. A rat sprung a trap and came at them, hissing, its haunches caught, dragging the thing down the hall. Glory days. Dirty dark-bar days. A mouse ran up Bird's sleeve and nipped her.

Her mother came to her in dreams. She was dead but in dreams, she lived.

I smell fire, she said, *your toilet froze. I made you my nice kitten soup.*

Her mother set a bowl down before Bird. The kittens simmered there, plump, unfurred—her mother always plucked them first, their bodies small as peas.

Her mother sang—the tune of the plastic shopping bag the wind had hung from a tree. Old winter wind. Old mother dead. Mickey slept and slept. Bird carried his child, tiny yet; they called it Caroline, little Caroline, which had been her mother's name.

Bird wrote notes to her mother then, in the months she lived in Brooklyn, as though her mother were still alive. She wrote: *I dreamed all the dogs I ever loved were running laps through the leaves around our house.*

She wrote: *I met a boy named Mickey. I crossed the room with my shoe off, my spiky heel, and knocked him between the eyes.*

He hooks his finger in my ear to kiss me.

He sleeps with his eyes open.

We call the baby Caroline, she wrote. *Sometimes Mickey calls me Caroline. I cut my hair like your hair. I still have all your dresses.*

She wrote: *His eyes are nearly white, Mother. It must be you love him, too.*

Bird is wearing her mother's robe even now, swabbing the sink, her shoulder hiked up to hold the phone. The house is quiet; the wind has quit. Everyone else is still sleeping. Even the dog is sleeping, stretched out on her side beside the woodstove, twitching through her dreams. Bird dog, Bird's dog, demoted the moment her firstborn was born.

The house is quiet, that is, but for Suzie. Suzie won't let her go.

"Hold on," Suzie says. "Don't go," and sets the phone down, and walks off to snort whatever she snorts these days in a room where Bird can't hear.

"Suzie," Bird says. "I hear you. I've known you for a thousand years."

The phone heats up, feels wet against Bird's ear—that's the burned-off waste of Suzie talking, Bird thinks. She's back from Fiji, Machu Picchu, back from Timbuktu. Patagonia, Rapid City, Ngorongoro.

"*Ngogn* was my boy's first word," Bird says, slides the word in edgewise.

Suzie doesn't miss a beat. She took a picture, she says, scuba diving. They were in a big pod of killer whales and the picture she took was black.

"I don't get it," Bird says.

"Black!" Suzie says. "As in solid? As in that's how close they came?"

"They're the only whale that will leave the water—"

"Yeah no, I know it. I saw, sugar. This one had a seal it snagged from the beach and bumped into the air like a kitten."

Kitten is a name for Bird's baby.

Ngogn is a word for dog.

"I'll let you go," Bird insists, and takes the first stair.

But something in her gives way.

"Bird?"

She has let a sound out. It is the sound of a woman run through. *Harpooned,* she thinks, *fructifying bolt*—right through the bony floor.

"Hurts," she says. "Hold it."

First stair. Seventeen to go.

Suzie's been up Cotopaxi, Aconcagua, Mt. McKinley, Rainier. Stuffed her foot through the sinking snows of the fabled Kilimanjaro.

"You going to make it?" Suzie says.

"I'm dying."

"You're killing yourself."

"I'm called."

"Every beat of the fucking day," Suzie says.

"So you said," Bird says, and they are finished, having come back around.

Bird hangs up and sits on the stairs still talking, wondering if it might be true. She might be dying, that is, or only making it up. There is a code she doesn't know, she thinks there must be, a sneaky, menacing tally. She lost seven teeth when she was pregnant—her gums withered, the yellow roots let go. She swallowed a tooth in her sleep one night and thought she had swallowed the baby, thought: I will have to give birth through my head.

"Like Zeus," said her husband, teasing, "weird god of the fructifying bolt," and walked out into the world.

What a fancy man Bird had married. Her boy calls him Fancy Man, too. Little Whale, White Moon, he calls the baby.

Bird cracked her pelvis, giving birth to that baby, and it hurts her still to walk. Not always, true, but all at once, going up. Plus the doctor had to go back in there—to get the last of the bone and the balled-up hair that the baby had left behind. Scrape it out.

Bird counts to ten—that helps—with her head down, sitting on the gritty stairs. Dog hair, dryer fluff—she doesn't clean much. She doesn't walk much. But she used to!

Bird takes the stairs the way she has learned to—sitting, moving backward, moving up, thinking of the seal and its flippers. Hands on the step: straighten your arms: hoist your big butt up.

She needs a bladder tuck—doctor said so. Her bladder sags, it pooches out of her—unmoored and inelastic—any time she stands. So she sits, and tests it with her finger, and of course she thinks *baby*. But this one will be pelagic and never come to land.

Bird reaches the landing and drags her mother's robe across a nail poked up from the wide-plank floor. A scrap of cloth tears free when Bird stands up, a ragged wing her boy will bring to breakfast in the flat of his hand, saying, "Mama, I found a, I found a, I found a—"

But it is not, after all, a butterfly like the one that once stood on his nose.

For now, he sleeps. The boy sounds like seven men sleeping. He is small enough Bird could carry him still from room to room to room, if she could.

He says, "Carry me like a baby. Feed me your milk like a baby. Feed me the kind that's cream."

She finds the rug with her feet, holds her hands out, blind, finds her bed in the dark.

"Who called?" her husband asks.

Bird doesn't answer him. He'll be down in a beat, in a long-drawn breath—a heavy sleeper, her husband, heavier since the children came.

Bird slides her cold feet into the heat he makes. She drops off to sleep for a minute, three, for a glimpse of a dream of Mickey, Mickey galloping over the prairie swinging a lariat over his head—roping gophers, roping coyote. *Ho doggie.* Not another two-legger in sight. But something whimpers, hurt, in the grasses, lost.

That's the baby startled awake in her crib.

Bird moves toward her, the sizzle of panic starting up in her chest: she is too slow, too late, she always will be. The baby sounds like a barking machine. She thrashes in her crib, unboned and blind, good as blind. The weight of her body pins her, strands her in the drift of her sheet: she's been dropped by the wind, breached from the sea. Shored up here, needing.

Every living tissue, Bird thinks. She doesn't want to, but of course she does. Bird wants a shirt that smells of her mother still to ball up in her hands. So to sleep. Sleep and let the phone go, let the school bus pass. Take the day in bed.

I can't want that.

But she does.

She brings the baby to her breast in bed and tries to sleep. Nothing doing. She's all stirred up. She smells smoke, or a hurricane coming. Smells the baby's milky head. She has a tooth already, this baby, a little headstone poking through. A little zing when she nurses. It hurts. If only it would hurt a little more, Bird thinks, maybe she would wake him. Take her man in her mouth and wake him, want him hard again. *Gimme gimme.*

She tries to want that, but what she finds to want is the mess of herself, the old dream that Suzie lives. Makes up, or lives, Bird cannot sort it. She cannot sort the news from the wishful, the actual from the dreamed-up muck of what Suzie fears, or Bird does, from what Suzie wants, or Bird does, or half the time what difference there is between wanting at all and fear.

She will turn a corner and find him there.

She will never in her life again see him.

Sacred, she thinks, and narcotic. That's how it felt to her.

And now every word Bird utters or hears makes it feel flimsy and dull. But it wasn't. It was sacred, she thinks, and narcotic. Doomed—but that didn't matter.

That Mickey lived for weeks in his ragtop—summer then, the sumac high, down by the Brooklyn Bridge. Didn't matter to her. They climbed the trusses—in the wind, the rain, the dark of the night they met. They were lit. They were lights in the great swag of lights the river passed beneath with its garbage scows, its freight of darkened souls.

They kissed, and the air everywhere went sparky.

Sparky is her boy's word.

May he never be a boy like Mickey was. May he never meet a girl the girl Bird was.

She draws the baby close against her. She can net her whole back with one hand. *I will keep you from anything doomed*, Bird thinks, and her heart picks up—with wanting, she thinks, and fear.

Appetite and revulsion.

Your life swings around, and you survive it. You make something other of it—life from life—keeping what you can. Even when you can't keep much.

She would never in her life again see him.

But she keeps cuttings of Mickey's hair balled up in a drawer somewhere. She keeps the peel of the first orange they shared and a cruddy bloody tissue. Not much. He had demolished everything else: the little clay pot he had made for her, the painting of a silver-lined cloud. He rode her bicycle into the river. Mickey burned every letter he had written to her and the box he had made to hold them.

The note he left said, *Forgive me. I talked to your mother while I wrecked that stuff. I don't know why I did.*

Of course Bird kept it.

The photograph of the dog in the ragtop, Mickey kept. He kept the photograph Bird took of her mother, newly dead, she had shared with him from shame: Bird's mother in her bed before the coroner came. She looked terrified. She looked to be screaming, still bleeding from her ears.

Of all the things Mickey might have kept, he kept snapshots of the dead. Think of that, Bird thinks—and count your stars. Count yourself lucky you survived him.

Or not. Because wasn't surviving the worst part? The dreadful onset of the cure? There was nothing you couldn't get over. You could sorrow all your life, but still you lived, you lived. You hoarded. You flew your mother on a string like a kite.

Of course it pulled. The kite was enormous. Her mother called down: it was lonely, dying alone.

But there was always more string to let out, Bird found, to keep from being lifted, to keep her mother lifting away. And Bird was heavy. She felt stuffed with sand when her mother died, the anchor and solace of grief. She couldn't move; she couldn't want to. Should she move, Bird moved against a current and the current wore her away. Even sleep wore her away: the dream that her mother still lived. Bird would turn a corner and find her still dying in some darkened room. Bird had forgotten her. She needed peanuts. She smelled of shit. She needed her ears to be cleaned. Daisies, she needed. Tchaikovsky. A nice bowl of kittens and peas.

I will never die, her mother insisted.

And died. And died again.

It would be years before Bird dreamed of her living, the months Bird carried her first child.

Second child, her mother reminded her, and came to Bird nursing the baby that Mickey and Bird had lost.

Don't suffer in silence, her mother insisted.

Don't ask is it a boy or a girl.

Don't eat around the thing you want most, her mother warned. *If it's pork chop you want, don't start with peas.*

Her mother sat in a chair and spoke softly. Not until Bird asked to hold the baby did her mother fly up on her string and grow small.

The spool for the string for the kite was red and shaped to hold as when riding a bike. The dream changed but the spool did not. Bird wore chartreuse or a bra and flip flops. They were seaside, or among the chalky cliffs of the desert, or on the rooftop of Furr's cafeteria, where Bird has never been. Bird could work that kite, no matter—reel it near to hear her mother whisper, let it out to let her scream.

Who will die when I die?

What am I to you?

Bird carried a rock in her pocket to remember she meant to live: at least she meant to want to.

I will be your age soon enough, Mother. I want to stay right here.

Where in the world, her mother asked her, *is here?*

She lifted Bird into the blue by the spool.

I want to stay with Mickey.

That's your Mickey down there, watching.

Bird's mother flew a loop above him and broke her daughter open on the ridge.

It was not sand that poured from Bird's knees as she flew but a thousand tiny kites of herself, as dry and light as leaves. Mickey ran circles to catch them.

They bedded down together—first night, the night they shimmied up the Brooklyn Bridge.

He had a flask they drank from, a packet of junk to snort. He rode her home through the dark on her bicycle, Bird on her handlebars shaking, the wet of his breath on her back.

"Turn here," she said and he didn't. He rode her to some-place he knew—a weedy patch on the riverbank, a dirty dark bar on Avenue B with songs he liked on the jukebox.

Love, love will tear us apart, the song went.

But it wouldn't. But it already was.

There was the way her back dimpled above the belt she wore and the heat of the way she smelled.

There were her hands, which to Mickey looked bor-rowed. His hands were shaped like Bird's hands. Their bod-ies fit together.

They danced in the dim reach of the bar in the dance that is like lying together, half a song, the unholy swoon of new humans falling into each other. They would never be more lovely.

When at last he rode Bird home on her bicycle, Mickey dumped it on a turn swinging off the bridge and they lay in the street laughing, gravel and a spatter of glass driven in under their skin.

"I love you already," she told him.

A car made the turn and missed them.

He said, "Oh, and I love you."

They had knocked the bike out of true and the wheel made a *shh,* a mother-sound, dependable as a heartbeat, all the way, all the way home.

Go home, her boy wails when the snowman takes the child's hand and flies north. *Go home, go home, go home.*

He is talking in his sleep down the hall—something about a spoon he needs and one last ravioli—a dream that has lasted all night. For weeks of nights he dreamed his dream of a bad underwater deer.

He's a messy sleeper, Bird's boy. He winds his sheet around his arms and feet and wakes himself by screaming: somebody tied him up. Or he's up and asleep and walking. He is peeing in the freezer. He opens a drawer in his chest of drawers and pees on his just-laundered clothes.

Bird's husband is sleeping softly, his mouth crushed against his pillow. *I choose you,* she thinks, and moves in. A good man. Dog and hearth and children, the lucky, lucky life they have—a life her mother lived. *I choose you.*

Fancy Man. She wants to smack him. She just could— for sleeping, say, while she isn't. For shedding a hair on her pillow.

So Mickey moved.

So what?

Thought to marry.

And if he did?

What if he went ahead and married and lived a life that looked a little like Bird's life? *Lived a lie,* she wants to say— it's not for him.

Suppose it is: somebody else would be in it. Prairie

Lee. Victorine. Not you, Bird. It isn't you, Bird: you've been married a dozen years.

So why wake to the man, mussed by dreams, the old miserable pinch and burn? Why wake to Tuk and Doll Doll and driving the Drive Away out—that old saw, the only story of them she would tell?

She used to tell the story to strangers, in a mood—tell it brightly, from a distance, her husband across the room.

"Three days from Denver to Pueblo," she said, "and then these two nuts in a Ryder truck—"

She would catch her husband watching. Was he proud some? Proudsome, pleased? She thought so. Pleased with her and with the part he had played: he had signed her up, smoothed her out.

Pleased and also sorry: had he not felt that, too?

Hadn't he wanted more of her, all the old somebody-elses she had been, the torn-apart feeling she hoards?

She blows a spider from her husband's cheek, a tiny golden fleck ascending its silver thread. Silver, the dew. The cows are eating windfall apples—beyond the window, beyond the sandbox and its rusting toys. Bird hung a swing in the tree—a rope with knots her boy jumped from and broke his arm on the first day of school. The rope bends in the wind, moves toward her. Swallows bicker in the eaves.

Hello, love, she thinks.

Hello, Mickey.

She lays her leg across her husband's knees, the seam in back where he is stitched together; she draws a knuckle up the groove of his spine. Feels the life in him and, reaching, reaches for everyone at once: her girl, and the boy who Mickey was. For Charlie and Jack and Vladimir, she reaches, Virginia and Horace and Fred.

A dozen years they have passed together. He is a book she once read. A dying painter. A woman waving goodbye in the street.

Goodbye, love, Bird thinks.

She feels her lung clap shut. That old sneak cat.

"Mama, stay awake with me, Mama. I'm afraid to close my eyes."

"I can't sleep, Bird. I'm sorry to wake you."

Trouble: she had seen him coming: *come here.*

He put his cigarette out in her layered drink and brought her to bed, too jangly to sleep.

"I keep thinking if I close my eyes I will never open them again. I'm sorry to wake you. I can't help it. I want to make you proud of me. I want to fuck you until you can't bear it anymore until you wear down and cry. I should let you sleep, Bird. Little sparrow. I'm sorry to wake you. I keep dreaming you are up on the bridge in the rain and the city is wet and blue. A boat is passing. I can't see your face. Everything is blue. You're all blue. It's beautiful. You are. And I'm in you. I'm in you and the boat is like a ghost of a boat and the stars are like snow but frantic and burning out in your hair."

Later, months, weeks, she didn't know, Mickey gouged at himself with a penknife.

Asked, "When do I get to kill you?"

"Soon, won't be long."

How they felt it. He meant it and she did too.

Lunacy, yes, stupid—but it had them by the throat, this idea, some spangly shock of narcotic they made, oblivion— out of nothing.

"When do I get to kill you?"

"What do I get to use?"

The answers came to them in the bedroom, sprung from the heat of fucking—bed talk, potty talk, not a plan so much as a feeling, needling, the watery sloppy hum and drift a grief in her, unhelpable. Something had to give. They would fly off a bridge, dusk coming down; they would slam the car into a wall. Nothing lasting. A moment's impulse, three.

Still an impulse: wasn't it as good most days, any old day, as intention?

The long grown list of intention, the hope of how to be.

Bird keeps grades on herself, the future school marm: a

B day, a D day, details her insufficiencies: too late, too late, forgot. Nice try! The costume hung together with straight pins, the sneakers at the bottom of the pool.

She tries the PTP, the LEC, the LCC—tries service, *attagirl*—all the ad hoc this and that. Nurses a tree in the churchyard. Nothing pure about it. She is balancing deed with the failure to do, hoping for a wash. She brokers her little mercies, pre-pays against calamity, the F and D minus days—thinks in averages, bigger pictures, the solid and sustainable C.

Oiled rusty bike chain

+

played guitar at All School

-

boy sears chin on cookie sheet

-

pup breaks neck on stairs

Bird wants to be caught. Flung out.

Her husband moans in his sleep, he twitches—a dog chasing squirrels in a dream.

Bird resorts to a different tally, to the one she keeps against him. For dreaming, for instance, when she isn't. For drinking the last drop of coffee. He never lets her use his toothbrush, or his 25-cent comb.

She wants all of it.

He tells her nothing. Tells her everything. Tells a good joke, his same good joke, and everybody laughs but her. Goofball, high school stories. Mellow man, man of good cheer. Easy to love, happy even asleep—but anything can be wielded. *I was happy and look what you did.*

"Did you see what I did? I washed the dishes. I fed the dog. This is me feeding the dog."

Bird loves him best in pictures, but what does this mean?

And why will he not take pictures—with the baby, her boy growing up? The irretrievable life unrecorded.

"But I do," he says. "I took a picture. Look there, there you are. There's your pretty boy. I took that. That's a nice little picture."

She bought a camera for her husband and he lost it in a week with seven shot frames inside.

Bird tried holding out her camera her arm's length away and aiming it down at the three of them, flat on their backs in bed. But she was pissy; she pouted, saw it each time: a woman giving grades out, a woman keeping score.

She'll get over it, fine. No matter. She will survive and die and her babies will live without a record of who they have been. Just as Bird lives. Doesn't matter. It is nothing but a life passing, a day smashed to golden shards.

Love, she thinks, *and duration.*

Sacred and narcotic.

You could fortify yourself against it. Hedge your bets; heed the signs.

A young man sleeps in a ragtop, for instance. Duct-tapes his sneakers together. His windshield is a patch of Lucite, stitched in, that whistles and thrums when he drives. There is a bullet in the defrost vent; a sack of bite-sized hamburgers deliquesces in the trunk. There are paw prints, handprints, smudge of a nose on each windowpane, the Naugahyde seat in shreds.

Think, girl. Read the signs.

She thinks of pictures they took—Bird of Mickey and Mickey of Bird. Bird slumped over the wheel of a roadster they found rolled into the weeds along the freeway. Her face wrecked, the windows webbed: Mickey's favorite.

Bird's: Mickey afloat above a trampoline, his hair staticked up, a dorsal horn, a boy in a cape, a man shrieking.

She hears her boy getting up down the hallway.

May he be a boy always like Mickey was.

May he wind a strand of hair around his bedpost.

May he sleep for months in a ragtop with the sumac high and survive it.

What an awful word—*survive,* Bird thinks. *Sufficient,* Bird thinks. *Service.*

Your porpoise is a service animal. Sufficiently intelligent to deactivate unwanted bombs.

This is before or after they are bleeding out their brains through their ears? Fucking Navy. Bird takes a short loop through her well-worn rant against the military-industrial complex—the terrors she scarcely thought of before she brought children into the world.

"You mean what's left of the world," Bird says out loud, and finds her boy at her shoulder saying, "Mama, don't be mad, Mama. There is pee all over my bed."

He bats at her face gently: that's an apology. Bird kisses his sweaty head. She rises with the baby still at her breast and steps into the moving day.

Bird is washing her boy's pissy sheets and stirring oatmeal on the stovetop when the telephone rings again.

Suzie again.

"Can't talk," Bird says. "I'm called."

"You dope," Suzie says. "I'm checking in on you. You okay? You won't be able to reach me. I'll be in the sack all week, sugar. My poet's up from New Orleans. It's all cocktails and crème brulee for us. I'm not budging to pick up the phone."

"I've been warned," Bird says. "That should do it."

"I mean it, sugar. You need anything? You sounded like you hurt."

"I hurt," Bird says, "and I improve. Every day by day. The bone knits up quite nicely. You?"

"Bruised," Suzie says. "Nothing broken. My ass is an unsightly yellow and my head is a little green."

"Your timing's bad."

"I should say."

"I'll let you go."

"I'm broke. I want a little dope for when he's here."

"That'd be nice," Bird says.

"We make our choices, I guess."

"And then we lie in them. I'm not floating you a loan."

"I didn't ask you to. I asked if you were okay," Suzie says.

"Well I slept and then you called and then I slept a little more. And then the baby waked."

"We make our choices."

"We do."

Bird thinks again of her husband sleeping, the warmth of his breath on his pillow.

It takes a funny sort of discipline to give yourself away.

Bird tries again to summon it and balks at the want for uncharted sleep while the sun swings under the world. But who sleeps anymore? Not even Suzie.

The phone rings in the dark. Suzie needs a ride from the bus stop. Suzie spent her last nickels on pizza. Suzie's new pal she's been sleeping with shoved her lightly on accident— *on accident*—down the stairs.

"But you should see him," Suzie says, "sleeping. He sleeps with his eyes open. He sleeps with his arms tossed over his head like a falling god. The moon is on him. It draws the tides in him toward the air—like dew, opened up, like he's blooming, like he is some succulent moon-white bloom dropped into my bed and lethal. I could tear him apart just to touch him."

"And he is what," Bird asks, "seventeen?"

"Newly carved. The boy glows like a skinned pear."

Bird's boy tugs at her robe. He needs her, it's true. He needs his blue socks. He wants that yellow hat with that M.

Bird wants the heart to hang up, quit—but she can't summon it quite, never has.

The morning is going. She finds the grooved spoon, favored. She ladles oatmeal over an army guy, a gluey mass, a joke he'll get, go, "Unh?"

He wants toast. He wants a little toast with syrup. May she make him a *dosht* with *seebup* and butter and one little dust of the cinnamon, Mama, "Mama, please, if you don't, will you please?"

"If I don't?" she asks.

"I will never say good night to you again."

"Are you talking to me?" Suzie wants to know. "I'm still here."

"Hold on, hold on," Bird says to both of them, and each of them says, "No way."

Her boy plunges out the door into the morning dew and appears again at the window. He grins, a mess, his lip is split, his teeth a train wrecked in his head. He licks the glass—there's an X—and is gone.

"I'm still here," Suzie says, "but I'm going, sugar. We may never speak again."

"Oh, quit," Bird says.

"I'm just saying."

"Well, don't," Bird says. "Take care of yourself, would you?"

"Oh, I do," Suzie says. "I take lots of care."

"Don't let your poet knock you down the stairs."

"Fool me once," Suzie says.

"Says the president."

"Remember that mother in Brooklyn who tripped going down the stairs—"

"Goodbye, Suzie."

"—and drove that pipe into her head?" Suzie says. "That was awful."

"Suzie."

"We may never speak again."

"You would miss my milky oatmeal," Bird says, stirring, "with the raisins plumped up just right."

"Your scraped toast I love."

"Exactly."

"The smell of fire in every room."

When it was summer still, days you could still ride a bike in your skirt or ride your girl around town in a ragtop, your dog; summer still, days kids bang the hydrants open and drive their bodies hard through the spray; Haitians on the stoop, hypodermics; music blaring up and down the street; summer still (*No Sitting Aloud*); White Castle burgers for breakfast (too hot to cook, too easy not to want to) for dinner, if they ate it, for lunch, for a time; days the ground-up mess of their haunches still healed from skidding out on Bird's bike in the street, the skin mounding over the glass they had picked up, tried to pick out, evermore would carry; days the willows in the park wore their hair down still for Mickey and Bird to lie under, in the sun should the wind allow it, in the shadows on their faces as they slept; before the nights cooled, before the first leaves turned, Bird and Mickey thought to find a place together.

They found a place burned up by a voodoo drummer who had left his candles burning. Cat tipped over the candlestick. The kitty litter ignited. The guy was banging his skins, meantime, at a fertility rite in Queens.

It was a step up, sure, from the ragtop. But the place was sooty head to foot when Bird and Mickey moved in, velvety with ash. Every room smelled of fire.

Bird's mother appeared and said: *Run.*

"Why slum?" Suzie said. "It's stupid. You could live uptown like I do."

"You could keep your feet in a bucket," Bird said.

But what Suzie said was true: they were broke but they didn't have to be. It was a thing to try. It was a badge of something, a feeling they liked—not to live every day a scrubbed-up life, sensibly decided, steaming on ahead. It was a way to keep things from happening: to be, and to hold themselves off from becoming.

Neighbor kids banged the hydrant open, summer days, and launched their bodies through the spray. The water seemed to drive clean through them. There was a boy Bird thought looked like Mickey as a boy—a skinny, noble, wild-looking boy who made her want to make her own wild boy and drive him far away.

Drive away, go away. We could, Bird insisted, even early on—before the signs coalesced. The trees were turning. The ragtop hadn't been towed.

Instead they scrubbed and scraped and painted, settled in. Bird took a job for a week and quit it—crumbing tables, some fancy joint. She wanted to keep to home. They built a bed from scrap. They found a table on the street and bought daisies and ate them, all but one. They threw sticks in the river for the dog to fetch, who fished out sheets of plywood, a boot, a mannish, ragged, woolly coat they dragged home for her to sleep on.

The dog slept underneath their bed. She whimpered when they fucked and clawed at the floor and bounded up and down the hall.

Run, her mother kept saying.

And Suzie said, "Why?"

But they liked it. The sun slid a finger through the alley, afternoons, and laid it across their bed.

"It's like food," Mickey said, and pushed her legs apart, "for your flower. Let me have a look at that flower."

And: "I looked in the mirror just now. I reminded me of you. Does that make sense? Do you see, Bird?"

"I can't see right," he said. "You make me dizzy and I want to fall down. I want to bite into your neck dust in your throat on my hand your blood on my cock and legs and I'm home sticky summer night, I am breathing your breath and you cry out and I want to fuck you so hard, Bird, now, now and for the rest of us living."

He fed her honey. Persimmon and chocolate. *Guess.* Silken lumpy cream. Mickey jabbed at Bird with the honey spout, drew a bead along her belly, up, like a suture that has risen and healed. *Be still. Be still.*

I want to see.

But they couldn't really—see. The world had shrunk by then to become them.

The wind picked leaves from the trees. Nobody walked the stretch they could see of their street. Nobody descended any longer in the cold on a thread to throw his bramble of sparks at the bridge. The river went its way in quiet, tugging garbage scows to sea.

They burned candles and dreamed of fire.

The cold pulled the color from the sky, the streets. The sun angled off for the season.

A band set up underneath their bed in the basement with the rats and the stopped-up john; they played sheet metal, paint can, pipe; the clacking pods of weed and tree. The sound was awful and the smell was worse: fat stools mounded and toppled in the john—the band members used the john like a bucket. The rats fled the basement and along came the mice with their paper scraps and hair they found and cobs of corn and chicken bones and they lived in the walls at Mickey and Bird's and in the dumbwaiter shaft. When the band played, a veil of paint flickered down from the walls.

Water streamed down the walls and from the ceiling when the up-neighbors filled their tub. The pipes leaked; the joists softened with rot. The voodoo drummer lived upstairs now and pulled his pod in the tub. They heard him grinding on his ass while the tub drained out, his baby in the kitchen, whimpering. He named her Precious—who had been squeezed out into life in that tub.

The mother cut the cord and swaddled the baby and left it in the kitchen sink. She had a bag already packed. She pushed through the door, tripped on the stoop, drove the shorn end of a railing pipe hard into her brain.

A clean bargain, a swap. No one spoke of it.

At last the days, grown cold, grew colder still. The band members cast down their instruments and went elsewhere to keep warm.

Good thinking, Bird thought. *Move along.*

But Bird and Mickey stayed put and watched the leaden skies of winter spit the first hard knots of snow.

When the shorn-off curls of the Hasidim boys came blowing down the street, Bird picked one out to ransom. A rat came to them, hissing, dragging the trap that had snapped on its haunches.

These were signs, Bird knew, legible enough, if a person meant to read them.

"We should go," Bird ventured, but they didn't. To go would mean something was over—that first bright febrile feeling.

Bird wrote a letter to her mother, and addressed it to her father, and stood in line at the post office to buy a tropical stamp. A man in his hat stood behind her, a stone in robes, a band of fur, his child in the carriage asleep. Bird was dressed in a breezy skirt. She dressed for the way the day had looked when she looked out through the window. She dressed for sun, for girls with chapping midriffs, for boys with no socks and shaved heads.

The man in his robes stood behind her, with his wife in her wig behind him, with next his sickly girls. His cane was polished. He used it to bring Bird's skirt up, thrust it between her legs. He tapped her once, tamped at her.

"Dirty goy," he whispered.

Dirty, dirty Jew.

Bird bought a pregnancy test on her way home. She would bathe when she got home and wake Mickey. She would run a bath scalding hot and listen for birds in the airshaft—creaking dullards that stayed behind when all the singing pretties flew south. He would feed her cantaloupe in the bathtub how he used to. And she would tell him. She would show him the stick she had peed on—the watery bands of blue.

Part way home, Bird broke into a run and ran past their stoop and around the block—once, and twice again. She was limber then, her blood moving. She would kiss Mickey awake and tell him everything she knew.

But he was gone. For days he was gone, no note that said where.

The note in the kitchen said: *Let me when I come home to you slowly unbraid your hair. Please please please please.*

And in the bedroom: *Please please please maybe marry me.*

Bird sat on the bed waiting, the pregnancy stick in his coffee cup by the bedside for him to find. If an ambulance passed, she pedaled after it to be sure it wasn't him.

It wasn't him.

A week passed, two. It wasn't him.

And then it was.

Contusions, concussion—they called Bird to come to the ER. Mickey had stepped onto an elevator that wasn't there and fallen three floors down the airshaft. He was sobbing when she got there: the doctors had opened him up, he swore, and found nothing but sticks and leaves.

"You'll be fine," Bird said. "It's all fine, you'll see. We could marry. I will never use your comb."

"We could what?" Mickey said, and Bird blurted it out— the news of the missing days: dirty Jew, cantaloupe, the stick she had left in his coffee cup, a baby, they were going to have a baby, how did that sound to him?

"It was dark where I fell," he told her. "I didn't know where I was. A day passed before anyone came. I didn't know would the elevator start up and what would happen if it did. I didn't like the pictures—what I looked like zapped, what I looked like crushed. I kept seeing you when you found me. I was bleeding. I kept moving away from my blood—it would conduct the charge, I decided. I'd be fried in a puddle of blood. Or I'd be saved, but when they hauled me up the cable to lift me out, I would pick up a fatal splinter, a strand worked loose from the braided steel that would sail through me like a spear thrown into the royal chamber of my heart. You're in my royal chamber, Bird. But my head feels broken open. Every word feels like fire I speak."

When they got back to their place from the hospital, the up-neighbors' tub had fallen through. With it came diapers and droppings, a bloodied tampon, a gnawed-on bone, a poisoned rat as long as Bird's arm with its eyes busted out of their sacks.

"That was lucky," Mickey offered, serious.

He was armored in pharmaceuticals, resplendent in the sun. Untouchable.

"Try to touch me," he said.

They hadn't been crushed, after all, by any of it—not by a rising elevator, not by a falling tub. Mickey brightened for weeks with the luck of it. He rubbed Bird's belly sweetly, speaking her mother's name. She would jump horses, their girl, as her mother had. She would play violin on a riverbank. She would know to fill a tub when the ice storm came and lay in wood and sit tight. She'd have hobbies—stamps and woodcuts, earrings of feathers and beads.

"Little Caroline, little Caroline," Mickey told her, "we will knit you a poncho each year. We will sleep out under the apple trees in spring when the blossoms blow down."

The days grew colder still. They dragged the tub into the bedroom at last and used it like a barrel to burn in—sticks and leaves and coconut husks and books they had read, to keep warm.

It is cold *where we are and quiet,* Bird wrote.

We will have to wreck one another, she wrote.

I am happier than ever, Mother, she wrote.

And: *I have never been so scared.*

"You scared?"

"You?"

"Maybe."

"No."

Mickey pressed a pillow against her face.

"Don't be scared, Bird. Do you want to die or live?"

When Mickey had healed enough to move again, before the Vicodin ran out, they rode bikes across the bridge in the drizzle to their dark bar on Avenue B. They were swacked before they got there and shaking with cold. In the warm, they drank and drank.

Bird knew better. The babies of drunks were lumpish. She knew better than a diet of White Castle and junk and Almond Joys. Sleep and greens, she knew, dark berries. You weren't ever to kill a spider those months or walk through a silver web. She hung their mittens; she kept their hats up off the bed. She kept their shoes switched and sorted for luck how her mother always told her, with the left shoe in the right foot's place, the right in the left, lined up. Little tricks—for slipping babies out past the gods.

But more than this, Bird worked to seem as Mickey mostly was: mostly she worked on forgetting she had a baby in her at all.

Their song was on repeat on the jukebox; the regulars sat their stools. It was warm inside, swampy almost—wet clothes and the heat of bodies. The bartender wore a shirt slashed across the back to let his tattoo show. An ampersand, the bartender's tat. *And* is truer than *but,* they agreed. They drank whiskey and felt exalted. Bird's flocked-around feeling had gone.

They pushed out of the bar and the spiderwebs, meaty-looking and clotted with dust, swung in the burst of wind.

The street was torn up. There were pipes stacked up on the sidewalk—spanking-new silver lengths of pipe big enough to creep in, light enough to roll. They crept into a pipe and lay flat—cramped twins, knotted up, minutes apart, their bodies the same size. The pipe hummed in the wind and sleet. Bird kissed Mickey and, on the count of three, they threw their weight to one side. Now they were rolling. It hurt—which was funny. To be stewed in the swampy heat of the bar and now thrash about in the cold and grit, the reverb bright and tinny—everything was funny. The pipe banged down off the sidewalk and onto Avenue B, easy enough, gaining speed. Whiskey made it fast and flashy. They bucked against one another, bloodied themselves on the ribs of the pipe. They saw a taxi whip past through the mouth of the pipe and streetlights, streetlights passing, an umbrella inside out. Mickey shouted something that sounded like *Wa Lou Re.* Which was funny. Dumbass kidstuff funny. A woozy, goofy feeling.

Worth it?

Naw. Maybe.

Worth a trip to the ER, worth a trip to the morgue?

Yeah. *Owright.* Maybe.

Wa Lou Re.

Now Bird could make him out. "Will you?"

"Yes."

"Marry me?"

"Yes."

"Will you marry me?"

"Yes, yes, yes."

They had spent all their nickels on whiskey so they wriggled from the pipe and flagged down a cab and bolted on the fare when they got home. They were wet to the bone and happy— hoped to sleep so, wake so, keep it. They kept out of range at the back of their place, leaning into each other, kissing, until the cabbie whipped a stick at their window and peeled off down the street.

They would burn a fire to warm themselves and sleep under a heap of blankets, the dog dreaming at their knees. But the dog didn't come when they called her. The dog had been hanged from the heating duct. The note was from the landlord: *you owe me four months' rent.*

Mickey lifted the dog to carry her, her front legs over his shoulders. He carried her like the sleeping child they were never going to have and laid her down on their bed to look at her and whisper curses in her ear. Toilet paper clung to her whiskers from drinking from the unflushed bowl. Mickey used Bird's brush to brush the dog and scraped her teeth clean with a key.

"Poor Maggie," he kept saying. "Poor, poor girl."

They took pictures. Her mouth stiffened into a nasty snarl they had never seen on her in life. Mickey rubbed at his face with her ear.

"You still smell like my Maggie," he told her.

At last he covered her with the rancid coat she had dragged like the dead from the river. Then he raged on the street until daybreak, smashing pay phones with a chair.

Glory days? Bird thinks. *Ridiculous.*

She is lucky to be alive.

The morning going. The baby hungry and still in her bloated diaper. What in the world did they make those things with, with their insides like plumped tapioca, to endure the next 400 years?

Endure, Bird thinks, *prevail.*

If you are truly mine in spirit, then you must prevail, her mother said.

There is a place you cannot get yourself back from and this is where I am. You will cut your hair like my hair. You will wear my pretty dresses. Your Mickey knows the way.

He wrote notes on the walls and mirrors.

Your friend Suzie called. She was snatched from the jaws of a hippo today. In Botswana, I think. Somewhere. An engine fell off a 747 today. No one was hurt. Kind of funny. I feel sick and scared without you. I have blood from you still on my hands.

And: *Going down to the corner. 3 a.m. See you soon. In about 147 hours.*

The day is blowing. The leaves flock down and shore against the barn, snagged up together, they twitch. They don't look right. They don't look enough like leaves.

Bird goes barefoot through the unhappy grass and finds her boy in the drift of leaves, his pajamas splotched with dew. He has dropped to sleep again, hiding, waiting to be found.

"Up, up," she says, and tickles him awake.

"Did you see your kiss on the goodbye window I left? I left you an X," he tells her, "for when I am gone to school."

"Come, sprocket," Bird says. "Hully up."

"Hully up, hully up, hully up," her boy says, dragging his feet through the dew.

His feet leave wet prints on the kitchen floor that won't dry until after Bird's husband is gone, after Bird calls Suzie and Suzie calls Bird and Bird is drunk with the baby and coming apart in the tub upstairs. The dog will drink from the tub while they are in it and lick at the steamed-up faucet. For now, the dog sleeps beside the woodstove. Family dog, dog of the marriage. No Maggie dog, this dog. This one sleeps the years away.

Her boy is reading *Babar* to this dog, remembering the words. His head on her neck for a pillow.

"She's dreaming somebody," Bird's boy says, "look—" and catches her tail she wags in her sleep.

The baby rocks in her singing seat, thumping softly at the dog's ribs. A tableau, a scene perfected, luminous and dear.

When my children were small, Bird will come to say, and the scene repeats in her head.

Bird's husband is still upstairs, hamming it up as he pisses, remembering mighty Achilles—fast runner, killer of men. Shit shower shave: the man will be down soon.

"If I got a gun and shot him, Mama, would it just be me and you?"

"Come eat," Bird tells him.

Bird's boy eats down to the army guy face-up in the mealy goo. He spoons the dude out and, with his crazy teeth, crushes his plastic bazooka.

"Those are keeping teeth," his mother reminds him.

"There's this kid who he hasn't lost even one. He still has all his babies."

The boy blows air up his sister's nose, who cries, having just gone quiet. It is not enough: he bites her cheek.

"Just you wait," he tells her.

He tries to wiggle her punky tooth.

"I wish I was still like you," he tells her.

"Shoes," says his mother, "backpack. Bus is on its way."

But does he move?

Nope—doesn't want to. He has grown up enough he has had the dream of reaching the schoolyard naked. He doesn't want to go. His stomach hurts him, he says, his head. His head feels like two heads, actually, and the front head is really small.

"Mama, can't I just stay home, Mama, and lie around with you?"

She keeps still for a beat to love him, loves him, a breath, like a lunatic, before she starts the push out the door. The morning hunt and gather. She finds his coat he flung under the trampoline, permission slips stuffed in the pockets. One glove. Some other kiddo's cap.

"Here go."

"No fair," he says. "It doesn't fit me."

He wants his socks that come up like. His handsome shirt, it's pictures. He wants home lunch. He hates raisins.

"Is this a raisin on my tongue?"

Bird holds a hand out.

"Spit. Now move along."

"Mama. Mama Mama Mama."

"Scoot."

"But really it is. It's pictures and something's gooey on my shirt."

Bird gives in. She stands guard at the end of the driveway while he runs upstairs for his handsome shirt. She listens for the bus to top the hill, listens to the baby cry. She is really belting it out, that baby. But Bird is standing guard. Bird has to flag the bus down. Bird is sort of resting, her mind a little gone.

Her mind is on the day her boy came home from school, first day, a hundred years ago, tattling on ratty Brody.

"Brody said the f word, I promise you he did."

"The f word?" Bird wondered.

"Yep."

"But what's the f word?" Bird wondered.

"*You* know. Frow up?"

"He walks in his sleep, the kid sleep-pees. He pissed last week in the freezer. Pissed in his papa's shoes. He lies on his back, spitting. Funniest thing you ever saw."

"He licked the cheese grater," Bird reported.

"Hit a home run."

"He hates me, he says, he loves me. He wants to stick me in the eye with a sword."

"*Pisgetti,* he says, and *gaky. Bumbanini* for bumblebee. A butterfly stood on his nose."

"I've heard enough," Suzie said.

"There's more."

The geese are moving. The town cat appears with a humming-bird clamped in its shiny mouth, the bird's spangled wings still shaking—some fickle godhead's sign. Bird feels her knees, unstrung; her throat seizes: she ought to keep her boy home from school. It isn't safe, not today. Does that sound right? She can't shake it.

It feels like mice, Bird's mother said, *nibbling at your throat, when something is on its way.*

On its way, Bird thinks, and so you watch for it. You put your shoulder to the wheel: you're a natural, babe. The model of the natural mother, governing by feel. You see it coming.

But if you don't?

Or if you do, and look away?

Because what about Calvin Coolidge? Bird thinks. What about his boy, a president's boy, playing tennis on the courts at the White House? Had there been a sign, some way to know, a feather on the wind, a spider in a hat? The boy blistered his hand playing tennis and from the blister contracted blood poisoning and from the poison was dead in days.

Crazy, the way things happen. Your life is charmed until it isn't, until a dark day that breaks like a dream.

Bird must have dreamed, to wake so shaken. The dream would come back to her. Something was in it.

Phooey, her mother would say, *let the boy go to school.*

Let the boy go get milk, Bird thinks—but it's the last thing you get to say.

Last thing the boy thought is maybe *Caroline.* Or: *I'll get me some Cheetos, too.*

Did that boy's mother—the neighbor boy's mother—have an inkling—something—anything—that he would shut the door behind him and never open it again?

A good boy, gone to fetch milk for his mother.

Bird can't picture him. She pictures the father. The boy's father strings flowers around the roadside oak the poor boy slammed the family Buick into. Bird sees the man as she saw him last: he walks on his knees, moaning, parting the skittering leaves. When he reaches the place where his boy died, the last place his boy once lived, the father throws himself onto the road. He presses his mouth to the asphalt and scoops up stones with his tongue. He must be waiting, Bird thinks, feeling it out. Lying in the road to divine the hum of what else is yet to be.

Bird's nearer neighbor tends to his garbage, sets his barrel of plastic aflame. Early at his chores, wheezing, standing fast in the acrid cloud—a man doing his part for the planet. Bird waves hello and curses him. Fondler of children, petty thief, a giant with a failing heart.

Fail better, Bird thinks. *Hully up.*

Mothers all over the country are waiting in robes for the school bus. Stirring oatmeal, scrubbing at knees. Rousing their gray-eyed heroes, fast runners, killers of men. Whilst.

Nobody gets to say *whilst* anymore.

The immortals are paring their fingernails whilst, landward, the great seas surge. The mountains burst and shudder.

Bird shuts her eyes and falls backwards. Whenever she shuts her eyes, she falls backwards, listening for her mother: *I am right here.*

Sparrows rustle in the wine-dark maple. Steam is lifting away from the road.

Here it comes: the school bus shrilling up the hill. The chain wound around the axle picks out its tinkling song. The bus grinds to a stop and the bus driver smiles—a pitying, reproachful look: Bird is in her mother's milk-sopped bathrobe still, and barefoot, and her boy is nowhere to be seen.

But Bird can picture him: thudding in a rush, his shoes

undone, down the pitch of the narrow stairs. She draws her robe across her chest and shuts her eyes. Bird stands in the road falling backward until the bus revs to roll away.

Hey! She throws her hands up. Her robe swings open, the color of a different day.

"Here he comes!" she yells, and he does—papers, cap, forbidden cards flapping out of his backpack. Toothasaurus. Cotton top. He's got his shirt a button away from being buttoned right.

"Farewell, my prince," she whispers.

Her boy climbs on and trots down the aisle, his quarrel with school forgotten.

Bird keeps standing in the road in her bathrobe in the doorway of the bus folded open—in the surge of heat, the smell of it, nothing smells like a school bus, nor a baby's head, nor a Band-Aid. *Thank you, Band-Aid,* Bird thinks, and backs off.

She waves at the bus until it tops the next hill and the last patch of yellow slides away.

She left the teapot on and now the windows are steamed.

The baby's shrieking. Her papa is singing in the shower upstairs.

He is closing in on the phase where he talks to himself, pulling on his shoes. Same shoes. He has bought the same shoes for three hundred years.

Meaning what? Bird thinks.

As in what?

Bird pours his coffee, nice of her, it will be just right to chug.

The day keeps changing: rain: and sun: and shadow. She should have sent her boy off in his frog boots. She sent him out fed, what a mama. Belly full of groats and a cracker.

The dog is licking at the baby's sleeper, the sack Bird puts her in. A good dog. If only she didn't shit, Bird thinks. If only she fed herself.

The dog turns to feasting on the mealy foam that leaks out of her bed. Her tail flares up against the woodstove.

Better build a fence around that woodstove, Bird thinks, and that awful rhyme about the ladybird comes around again.

Doll Doll comes around again, too. Doll Doll with her beautiful baby teeth, neat and straight and small. Milk teeth, deciduous teeth. Not your keepers. Passing through. She had skin like melted plastic glommed onto her neck and arms.

"What's that smell?" her husband calls down. "What are you burning?"

"Don't worry. It's only the dog."

"Stupid dog."

I never wanted her.

I never did want that dog.

"I killed my fucking dog," Mickey said.

"But you didn't," Bird said.

"But you didn't," Mickey mocked her. He took a swing at the wall.

"I was out getting drunk with you," he said. "Why was I with you?"

"Mickey, stop," Bird said.

"I don't mean it." He picked a chair up and poked her in the stomach. "We don't mean it. We don't mean anything. Keep away from me, Bird. I'm not well."

"You're not well," Bird said, and moved toward him.

Make yourself large, her mother had taught her, should you meet a sneak cat in the woods.

Sneak cat, cougar, puma.

Hold your hat in the air and sing to it until it turns to go.

Mickey passed the night smashing pay phones and came back to Bird worn out. He was carrying an armload of daisies; he had stuffed the dowels of the splintered chair into his pants. The dog was still laid out on the bed. She had begun to bloat; she was leaking—in death as in life, only more.

They cut her dewclaw away with a tin snip and the last little bone of her tail. They used the coat she once dragged from the muck as a sling and carried her down to the river.

The day broke leaden and gray. They tossed the yellow-eyed blooms into the river, one by one: *loves me,* saying, *loves me still.*

When the current took the last bright speck, they bore the dog over the bank and in in the rancid coat she once slept on. They went to their knees in the water. Mickey laid his gloves on the basket of her ribs; Bird laid her little hat. They tried an anthem—for spacious skies, a fruited plain. Garbage clogged the little eddy they stood in and ice had begun to form.

The coat was like a raft the dog slept on. The current tugged at the coat and they let go. She sank fast when they let her go.

But that wasn't how they told the story. She floated briefly, how they told the story, weirdly, on the little raft, on the pull of the seabound tide. A god had stretched out his hand above her, buoyant in the shadows of the bridge they had climbed, the bridge the poets leap from, the great swags hanging down.

"Brush my hair," Bird asks her husband. "Will you?"

He has a go at it, briefly, going easy in the shallows, keeping away from the knots below.

"Pretty," he says, so she won't cut it. He is sentimental and superstitious. He marks Bird's braid with his finger, saying, *this much you grew while my father lived. This much you grew in Paris.*

Irregular, his reckoning, his calendar approximate. This is the month the Poles rode out, with sabers, against the German tanks. About now was the Norman invasion.

When peepers begin in the swamp behind their house, so, too, begins the season they married. Born in the spring and married on the day his father died. He marks the morning hour his father—alone in the desert, far from home—dropped in a burning airplane out of a spotless sky.

He plucks a strand of hair from the hairbrush and holds it over the flame until it shrinks to a ringlet of ash. He tries another, curious, so long as Bird's back is turned.

"I smell fire," Bird says and finds her husband feeding the wavering flame.

"Very funny," Bird says and bumps him, "and wicked very smart."

"You widiot," her boy would say, quick to side with her, if he were in the house to side with her and not in that stupid school.

He would say, "One time I had a dog named Maggie. She flew her ears in my ragtop. She took down my mama's hair."

"No, no, really, it's true. This is when I was grownup," he would say. "This is when I was in crush with you a million million times."

He will plunge off the bus with a sign, soon enough: *Mama I mist you in skool.*

Bird means to pick herself up by the end of the day, she will have to. For her boy, she will. But for now?

Her husband is showered, cheerful, combed. He is loitering in the kitchen with his trousers pressed burning strands of Bird's pulled-out hair.

He chugs his coffee, and stages the grownup re-make of a schoolboy's hunt and gather, talking as he goes.

"I got my keys, okay, I got my glasses, talked to Mother in the can, she's fine."

He is goofy a little, too happy by a lot. He takes his big-man strides, preparing. "Wallet, gym bag, watch, what else?"

The sun is on him: a man taking on the day.

Bird takes a seat in the ragged chair and makes a curtain of her half-brushed hair. She bends her face to the baby, nuzzles the baby's belly, wets the baby's pilly sleeper with—

"What, Bird? Those are tears?"

"You've had a dream," he says, "you can't remember. But it's got you all torn up."

"You need food," he ventures. "Talk to me. I should have poured your coffee. You want me to brush your hair."

He keeps at it—he can't leave until he has signed her up.

"It's the dog. You think the dog has Parvo. Have you gotten her shots for Parvo? I think she might have Parvo. Could be she needs her Parvo. Do you think she might be due?"

Helps her get her mind off.

Hiya hiya hiya yeah yeah yeah.

This is your wife with her mind off.

This is the little tissue I kept.

This is the dog the landlord hanged who we took away down to the tidal strait and threw in daisies after. Mickey and I did. You know Mickey.

"You look blasted," he says. "What is it? Free radicals in french fries? Emissions tests and taxes? Sunscreen in aubergine, in mist and stick and tube?"

"Or it's me," he says. "Something."

"Hush."

She passes her husband the phone book. Baffling to him, a phone book. He can't think what to do.

"The dog?" Bird says. "Parvo?"

He backs away some, shoulders his satchel. Wise move. The baby bubbles and hums.

"Lyme's, could be. Heartworm? She needs her DTP?" Bird says.

Stay, she thinks, and drives him out.

Thinks: *How about a week in bed, cowboy? Crème brulee and cocktails? Rose petals floating in the tub?*

Bird is holding her breath, hardly knows it. Her husband settles his glasses on the bridge of his nose. He looks shy almost, smiling sweetly. He gives a little shy-boy wave. Turns away.

The sun flares in the window. The nose of the lock slides home.

"We drove a Drive Away out," Bird announces, fogging the X her boy left on the window glass.

"I saw a bag of bread on the freeway," she shouts. "A little flock of shoes."

So long, so long. Farewell, my prince.

They are gone now and now she can miss them.

Now she can miss herself—who in the world she has been for her husband, who she meant to be to love.

The baby as a littler baby, her boy trotted off to school. Her mother dead, a broken doll, geese scudding down on the pond. Bird misses everything at once. One thing makes her want all the others—lived or not, still she misses them. She misses lives she has never lived—days issued out of the future, hours that will never be.

Bird misses her mother. Kisses the baby. She is a dead baby's mother. She will be her baby's dead mother, by and by, and her baby will be a dead mother, too. By and by. Best case, the gods willing.

Bird can see right out to the end of herself: out to the satiny coffin, her children gathered around. She sees them saddled, grown, old orphans—ranting the way she hears herself rant about the lunacy of the news: the frothing for war, the oceans ruined, the babies swiped and murdered. The talk people talk. The daily terrors. The whales deafed, the quiet boys freaked on psychotropics. *I want that one. I want you.*

Columbine. Turpentine. Pretty little place near the mountains.

I want your old place in Brooklyn with screw eyes set in the floor. How about?

Before they hanged the dog? Before the baby we lost?

And you can find my mother's scarves smelling of her still. And you can call me Caroline. Before our little Caroline? Welcome home, little chicken, little bird.

Bird sinks into it, a bloom of heat, so to feel it: the door swung to, the shrinking stars. A leaf falling. The way her mother spun her ruby on her finger, think of that. The way Mickey hooked his finger in her ear. Berries in the bathtub. Sweetened ferns. The sound of the chain on the asphalt road that the school bus drags behind it. Shall.

A swell of things: gathered, unsortable, gone.

Bird misses the one-ton they slept in, the rocks her husband used to bring to her from the places he used to go.

Salt pillars and clouds. The tamarack needles blown.

"I had a toothache," Bird says—too loudly, and to whom?

"He chewed up a grape for a poultice. He broke his hand slugging a wall."

Bird carries the baby upstairs. She lays the baby down on the bathmat. Walks out.

Out and back and is gone again. Down the stairs for a cup of rum—half a cup by the time the tub fills. Hot: she wants the heat to sink into.

They sink in. The baby moves through her private baby-phases of alarm and bliss.

"Boo," says the baby, then "booa," a plea, and snatches at Bird's breast. The left, the right, the foremilk, the hind.

I want that one.

"Say may I," Bird says. "Say please."

It won't be long, it never is. Please and thank you. Soon: *Actually, I want that and that one then and could I have that one again? Puh-uh-lee-zah?*

The baby's nursing, which makes Bird weepy.

Somebody quick say why.

They move from tub to rocker, the rocker beside the window, the bus whistling down the hill.

I want that one.

Wasn't that how it felt—not so long ago—looking out over the Lucite bins where all the born babies in the hospital slept or were fed or cried?

That one.

"When I was a born baby," the baby will come to say. "When I was a baby that died."

I want that one.

Say may I. Say please.

Bird thinks of Doll Doll—picking pups out, picking

Tuk. Of picking Mickey, Bird crossing the room with her shoe in her hand. *I want that one.* Bop you between the eyes.

Get your lucky bone out, get your talisman.

That one there is mine. This one?

In a mood, Bird is, wanting. Like to take off. Like to scream.

She took her babies out to Coney Island, to the aquarium there beside the sea. Her two.

Used to light out. Ride out there with the dog, she and Mickey. Let the dog swim. Come the cold months. Get in under the boardwalk, let his pants down. Smell the sea. Little bit. Sit out on a towel by the water.

I want that one.

Sweet time. Sweet little way of living.

She's got the *more* always, got the *gimmes*. Wants the old life, wants the new. All the many dips and surges, she wants, the stations of alarm and bliss. The luxury of a day to kill taking a bath with the baby. Kissing on the baby. Kissing her fancy man. Four days, she wants, in bed with him, every meal delivered. Créme brulee and cocktails. Wax paper packets of junk. Have a romp. Ask it in—all the old somebody elses they have been, everything they hoard.

Quick now. You fly through!

Waaaa. Nothing but heat and sunshine.

Come the cold months, nobody out there. Come the sunshine beside the sea.

She gets the tab of Mickey's zipper down, gets the button

slipped out through the buttonhole and she can't see him yet, she waits to see him, she waits, and he is rising up. *Oh, hi.* Lifting out of his britches. *Pleased to see you, sir. Hello, hi.*

I want that one.

Who boy. Boy do I, Bird thinks.

She kisses the baby's toes. The bottoms of her feet, wrinkled from the tub, her little wrinkled hands. Bird dresses the baby in her sparkle dress, her little beaded shoes. Props her up among pillows on the couch, takes a picture. Takes a dozen more.

The day passing. *Pfft!*

She goes through the Family Album, the snapshots buckled and blotchy between the plastic sleeves. They are orderly, chronological; she has sorted them some by color. Not the old life, but the new. Not the wedding, even, but the babies. Everything else is loose—Bird as a kid among horses, the snapshot of Mickey's dog. The picture she took of Tuk and Doll Doll, Doll Doll on the hood of the Ryder truck with bobby pins in her hair. Her legs bloodied. Her belly rounding up under her culotte.

A mess. The passing of years unrecorded—but Bird records them now.

This then this then this then this. Turns the page.

She finds the one of her boy at Coney Island, the aquarium there beside the sea. Belugas turning circles in the murk, the tank Lucite so they can see.

"They are watching a movie of us and we are watching a movie of them and everybody's happy," her boy had said.

And it was true, or could seem to be true: the whales had smooth impish faces. They were at play, smiling through the murk, coming around again.

They were never going to get very good at that part, Mickey and Bird weren't: at coming around again. Not at once, she thinks, not together. Not a movie to take your children to, nothing to show your ma: the little gougings, the wreck of the way they lived.

Hot blue bramble of welder's sparks. A boat passing. Everything is blue.

Pretty yourself how you used to, Bird. I'll take you back to Paris. I'll take you to Timbuktu.

Bird slips her hand between her legs and sees his face again. So quick the heat, sweet wandering star that blasts apart in her head.

But something's ringing. It's the phone.

Let it go. It rings again.

That will be Suzie, Bird thinks, but it isn't. It's the vet with his friendly reminder: the dog is due for Parvo, Lyme's, the whole panel, DTP.

"Can't get there," Bird tells him, "no car."

A lie. Because who strings flowers around roadside oaks

dizzy mothers slam the family car into, driving drunk with their babies at noon?

"As you wish," says the vet. "But she's due. Overdue, actually. I showed you the heart with the heartworm, yes?"

"Oh yes," says Bird. "Awful."

And hangs up.

The dog is gazing at her with its milky eyes. A good old dog, a layabout. You can forget she is even here. She'll die quietly, Bird wagers, beside the woodstove, considerate to the end. Bird will have time to dig a grave for her before the kids scrabble off the school bus; she will chink words into her headstone: *Never to Walk in Sunshine Again.*

For now the dog burns her tail calmly against the buckled wall of the woodstove: dog of their New England hills. Of their quieting life—no Maggie.

Maggie made herself known every minute. She pawed at your feet if you forgot her.

Maggie jumped up to take down Bird's hair. She hooked the hair band with her eyetooth, snuffling, tugged the band free and stood there rolling it in her mouth. You couldn't talk with that dog. How they said it: You can't have a conversation with that dog. She whimpered and paced and stewed.

Poor Maggie.

Gone But Not Forgotten.

I Was out Getting Drunk with You.

Mickey took to sleeping through the morning. He fell off the bed and kept sleeping through the brief green afternoons.

He would come around, Bird thought, he had to. Give him a little time.

Give him time. Given time. Give me time. Forgive me time.

Amend me my misliving.

He quit touching her. It was all he could do to look at her.

"I seem to suffer too much. I can't say why."

The chair Mickey smashed into pay phones the night they found Maggie hanged from the heating duct, Bird kindled stick by stick in the bathtub. They burned what was left of the books they had read. Books they hadn't.

Bird fished in a wind for garbage to burn, from the stream blown down their street. On a frozen wad of newsprint, a street collage, among the usual ads—Biggie Size your Coke (*piggie* is what her boy says, *You want to Piggie Size your Coke?*), the gimme sheets, the gotcha, the Last Days, Everything Must, Any Midwinter American Meal, was an ad for getting out. Gas money, hotel nights. They would pay you, even, to do it—to drive a Drive Away out.

Bird came inside from the brace of cold and shook Mickey awake and kissed him. Brought him his steaming coffee. It wouldn't matter where they went.

Of course it would. Bird wanted sunshine, a generous

sky. She wanted to see the monument of Crazy Horse, his arm as long as twelve elephants, thrust out over the plains.

"What do you think?" she asked Mickey.

He thought nothing.

"We can't stay here," Bird said. "We have nothing to eat. The toilet froze."

The baby was as big as a walnut now, as a tiny frog, slow in the cold.

He wouldn't budge.

Love. Love was impossible.

"I have a narrowing sense of joy and somehow I blame you," he allowed.

At that, Bird left the bedroom and the bit of heat it offered. She sat on the floor in the kitchen and stroked the newspaper smooth to read. She picked through last year's leaves, dismissed by the trees, a few still supple and red. She found a bone, bitten clean, and she bit it. She found her wad of curls shorn from Hasidim boys and picked one out to ransom.

They were killing each other. She could see that. She would have to save herself and go.

But Bird was better at staying than going. She could conjure every sweetness still—it was all tucked away in her head.

One last time, she thought—and got right into bed. She kissed him everywhere she could think to. She licked him between his toes. She breathed into the loops and channels of his ears. She wore him down, in short, with every tenderness that was hers to summon.

They slept afterwards and dreamed the same dream, which is one of the gifts we are given when we are sharp enough to know. They slept touching, and the dream-story shuttled between them, reckoning by friendly stars. The moon passed its light through the window.

It was the light of the moon Bird saw by when she waked, mercifully dim and blue. She waked screaming. A corkscrew was turning in her navel, how it felt, and their bed was soggy with blood.

Mickey didn't wake right away; she had to shake him. Their phone was cut off so they bundled Bird in the dog's old hairy blanket and went down the stoop into the street. The blood kept coming, pleasant almost, warm at least, for a minute. She wished he would carry her, but this was silly. The bodegas were closed, the pay phones smashed. There was hardly a car on the street. At last a cabbie stopped, took a look at Bird, and peeled off.

By the time they got to the ER, Bird was shaking with cold and delirious. Mickey had tried to carry her. Blood was matted in his hair, streaked across his face, across Bird's face, the mark of the dream they shared. Bird whimpered and talked to her mother. She wouldn't talk to Mickey or look at him. The room flew up if she looked at him and whipped around her head.

They knocked Bird out to finish up with it, the old D & C, the flush and suck, dilatation, curettage, good to go, up and out. She could have watched if she had wanted but she didn't. Mickey walked her in in her paisley shift, in stages helped her lie down. A gentle man, good to her. Loving of the lesser animals, good to her and kind.

They would find a way to speak of it. He would tell her in bits when she wanted to hear and stop should she ask and she didn't. She waked and slept and when she waked at last, the day was lifting and blue. She kept her head turned away and said nothing. The sun blazed through the murky window and blotted out the room.

When she spoke, it was to say she was ready to hear whatever Mickey had seen. Hear it all, she insisted, and be finished with it—Bird who was finished with nothing.

What was left was all tatter and thread, he told her. Broth and a bloody dumpling that caught and flinched in the tube.

"The tube?" she asked. "No, don't tell me."

How the brew splatted out in pickle jars, he told her—*tickle jars* was what Mickey said, by accident. Everything about it was accident, wantonness, and they laughed at the slip out of habit—hard for a beat and then harder until Mickey couldn't quit.

Bird hung back and watched him. She thought, *Here is a man drowning, a boy going hopelessly down.*

They had set her big feet hard in stirrups: same for the dead as for the living.

"This will hurt," she remembered. "You're going to feel a bit of a—easy—a bit of a—pinch." Yes. How they said it.

A pinch, a breeze, a prod. A leaf on its back with its feet in the air blown dryly down a road. Sort of that. They thought up things to say sort of about it.

"Time to go to the butcher," they said, and after that they said nothing at all.

They found a booth in back of a coffee shop, a heater working feebly against the season. Bird pulled her chair up to it; she was cold and she couldn't get warm. She tossed toast crumbs into the vent to burn and fed it strands of hair. Bird thought to call Suzie, but Suzie was elsewhere. Suzie was straddling an icy crevasse, rappelling down a palisade of stone. Suzie was hang gliding, *you should try it, sugar,* off the highest live volcano in the world.

"We lost our little Caroline," Bird told the waitress when she came. "We had a baby and now she's gone."

Mickey was gone, too. Bird didn't know where. She couldn't think how anything happened.

"Did he tell you what I should do?" Bird asked the waitress.

"He said to wait here."

Bird had made a mess on the bench she was trying to hide.

"Not to worry," the waitress told her. "He'll be back, sugar."

Nobody called her sugar but Suzie.

A whale is closer to a camel than to a fish, sugar.

Bird would never speak to Suzie again.

The bench was Naugahyde, a mottled red, the whole world should be red when you are bleeding. Bird lay down on the bench as if into the blood she had lost and sleep carried her away.

The place was closed by the time Bird waked again, but the waitress was still there, talking to Mickey. Bird feigned sleep and watched them.

If you touch her, Bird thought, *I swear to you*—but she couldn't think what she would do.

She half knew where she was. She raised her head and knocked into the table and her hair hung up in the flashing that prettified the rim.

"Hello, sleepy," Mickey said, and walked Bird through the snow to the buckaroo's car they were to drive across the country to Cheyenne.

He opened the door for Bird. "Nice rig."

"I'll drive."

He had smoothed a garbage bag out for Bird to sit on. He laid the seat back for her; she bumped it up again. She cranked the heat to high and they turned for the west, toward the last light leaving the sky. Three exits, a bridge, and they were lost, making hard blind turns down quiet streets, squinting into the snow. These were streets without even bodegas, block upon unlit block in collapse, a maze swept of anything living. The snow floated up, spun among leaves and wrappers in the piddly light their headlights cast: the world was flat after all, flipped over, repeating its small features. Bird was queasy; she leaked. Her head was still a mile from her feet and wind blew lightly through it.

"I give up," she said, pushed the words from her mouth.

Bird was asleep before Mickey found a road out and slept through dark and daylight; she waked to a stubble of corn on the plains and the slow-swung heads of oil wells, glad for the clean rim of the land, glad at last to see. She saw the Cross of the Plains in a bean field, the wing—ripped free—of a Cessna lashed to the bed of a truck.

She said, "My mother appeared in a box in my sleep to bring me a loop of pearls. Quick: before the doctor found out who she was. He was handsome, they are always handsome, with a ringlet of hose and a scissors."

They had scraped the mother in Bird out. Her mother was tiny, Thumbelina, set out on a rind of lemon across a bloody stew.

They drove dirt roads, a farmy grid, the houses high and white.

"Slow," she said, "I want to see."

A boy sat a log hung from a rope from the generous branch of an elm. Mickey stopped the car; they rolled their windows down. The day smelled of willow and grass, the grass brittle and furred, palomino.

The boy's sister wound him up by his knees. It wasn't winter here yet; they had thrown their coats to the ground. A last leaf rocked down and the boy lunged at it and swung his good leg up. He had lost his other leg at the knee. The boy's sister wound him up on the swing, away from her, into the paltry shadows. He was a long-haired boy and his hair was loose and in his teeth was a grass blonde as he was.

"Far enough," he said, "too far—"

No bigger a boy than Bird's is. His voice bellowed in his chest like a man's.

The boy's sister let loose and ducked away. He spun slowly at first, and faster, and the more he spun the faster he went, the more spinning pressed him out. His neck showed, a stalk, brockled and thin. His head seemed barely hooked to it and his hair, as if pulled, streamed out. He blurred, a body churned to butter.

The sister hopped from foot to foot; she babbled. The sound she made made two sounds, knocked from the flat face of the house. It ran its course through corrugate fields, the furrows at the sky converging like paths of a fine-toothed comb. She snatched her brother's hair as he passed and this slowed him, jerkily, and dragged him askew on the swing. She tried to help him; his foot struck her in the mouth. He was coming off the swing. Cripple boy. The log was tipped; the stub of his leg was off it. He hung against the rope holding on with his hands and the rope, unwound, wound up again, according to the laws of motion. The rope thickened with his hair. It wound up with the rope until he hung by his hair, a carnival act, an object still in motion, moved by the fact of its moving, spinning itself out again. His foot flopped about below him and caught his sister in the mouth again.

"Remember the bar on Avenue B? Remember the pipe we rolled in?" Bird asked.

"It wasn't so long ago. I do, Bird."

He had asked her to marry him. It seemed impossible, marriage, anything at all.

"He stepped on a fishing hook," Bird said. "It broke off in his heel. He didn't tell his folks, he was afraid to. He told his sister because nobody listens to her, not even the mother," Bird said.

"There's no mother," Bird said.

The father was starting across the field with a pitchfork. He had let the door to the house slap shut and the girl twitched, startled, shot. You could shoot her again and again, Bird thought, and still she would refuse to die. She was burbling.

Lunacy made her invincible. She was to blame for nothing.

"He couldn't get his foot in his shoe," Bird said. "The poison was running up his leg—bolts of yellow, bolts of blue. Too late," Bird said, "end of story."

"Think so?"

"I do. It's the old *too late*. Quiet and slow and deadly."

Bird picked up a rock and threw it and a hot little fibrous grume of blood slid into her pants again.

"You asked me to marry me," Bird said. "I mean you."

She was crying again, quietly, her hair falling over her eyes. Mickey moved off; he had her hand in his hand. The girl was hidden away in the grasses, her brother above her turning, still hanging from the rope by his hair. A tableau.

The father had nearly reached them.

He was jogging now with his pitchfork, shouting, "Who the hell are you?"

They drove on. Interstates and dirt roads. Hay packed away in great round bales, wind rolling over the prairie. They saw the salt pillars in Kansas, strange and unadorned. Rock fence posts. Double rainbow. They had a route they were told to follow that they followed not at all. They saw Crazy Horse rising out of the plains, out of the town of Custer, named after Custer; they saw the fort where Crazy Horse died, a prisoner held by his people, by Little Big Man, Young Man Afraid, while Private Gentles ran the bayonet through him.

"Cheer up, baby sweet. I wish you could," Mickey said.

Bird didn't want to—not yet. But soon. The country was working on her, the low rose gone to russet, the high bright move-along clouds. She was hungry again and gorged herself on chicken fried steak and Skittles, on vermilion faces of canyons, cliffs you could dig with a spoon. Bandolier, Mesa Verde, Chaco canyon—this was her girlhood, her blood's country, the great dry American open.

"Open up," Mickey said, and she did.

Cantaloupe in the bathtub, love, the curtains drawn, the heat blasting.

"Feed me to the furnace when I die," Bird said, "and leave a little bit of me here—" in the bed, she meant, of the Super 8, exit 42 off the interstate, where the mirrors come down off the wall.

They were days late, dollars short, by the time they got to Cheyenne, but the Drive Away clerk didn't care.

"You look happy," she said. "Where you headed? I bet you don't even know."

Which was true: they didn't. The clerk was headed down to Denver. She would take them south if they wanted.

"It doesn't blow as hard in Denver," she said. "I had a friend had a car door blow shut on her here and it broke her leg in two places."

"How you tell a tourist from a local?" she said. "A tourist chases his hat."

"I don't get it," Mickey said.

"In the wind, babe. When the wind picks his hat off his head?"

She sort of socked him in the arm, flirting.

"What's the difference between a rancher and a 747? When it sets down in Honolulu, a 747 quits whining."

"That's a good one," Mickey said, and socked her right back.

She told jokes all the way to Denver, not a one of them better than these.

"Who's the best baby on the planet?" Bird asks. "Think: princess with 49 dresses. Little Miss sparkly shoes."

The baby is like a doll Bird dresses who cannot quite sit up. She would do better, like as not, in the sea. Little guppy.

"Silly, guppies don't live in the sea," Bird says.

Bird is cleaning, sort of. She sweeps. She spits on a stain on the kitchen floor and rubs the spot clean with her sock feet.

What in the world, Bird thinks, are your sock feet? Hers are filthy; they'll do.

Bird slides her feet into her husband's boots and sets off down the road with the baby breathing sweetly against her chest. The geese are moving.

So soon? Can't you stay?

What if she had stayed in the west, Bird thinks, with Mickey, out in the dry wide open?

Yep. And what if the moon were cheese?

And what if they made you president, Bird, or better yet, the Queen?

She'd raze the suburbs, give it all back to the animals, open the gates of the zoo.

Was it true there was a zoo of good Christians to prove God's impeccable design? Better throw the bolt on that one. Those people need to die. She would line them all up—the CEOs, the greedy guts, the poachers, the cheats. Let the hyenas have at them.

Now there's a sport for your networks, yup. Let's get rid of the buttons and levers, return to hand-to-hand. It's just you, High Sir, and the hyena. You get a stick. The hyena gets a loop of your colon to unspool you by. *Now run.*

Nice, Bird thinks, and you're a mother? You keep the tally for the PTP?

The neighbor is still burning plastics: throw him in. Quick. Let his ticker quit.

I'm sorry, is what she means to say. Sorry, sweetheart, about the elephants. About the sea turtles with their heads lopped off, and the friendly, machine-gunned whales. About the owls, my love, and the antelope. About the drowning bears, the baby seals clubbed, the cormorants grounded by oil. About that wall we threw up to keep the Mexicans out across a migratory pathway millions of years old. For the sharks, finned and starving. Sorry. The food riots. The refugees. Dioxin in Mama's breast milk, sorry. Mercury in tuna; chickens with their beaks cut off, fed their own shit from a tube. It's cheap. It's worth it.

Sorry, love.

Welcome to the world.

"What's left of the world," Bird says again, second time today.

They walk the loop: neighbor, neighbor, sugar house, pond. Pretty little pond you can't swim in. You'll come out with an extra nose.

The baby's happy. *How did I get such a happy baby?* Bird wonders.

Blue blue day, bit of sunshine. The legendary leaves.

They are watching a movie of us and we are watching a movie of them and everybody's happy, Bird thinks.

White whale. The same eye sweeping past, not so different. Small. The dark clear curious orb.

Now there's a word, *orb,* you don't hear every day.

Dropped your orball. I kin get it.

The town cat, killer cat, rubs against Bird's leg.

"You want my happy baby, don't you? You can't have her, not in a million years."

In a million years, Bird thinks, what will the planet look like? What, in another ten?

She walks on, feeling lighter, sobering up. She shakes out her shirt in a sunshiny field and they lie on it, Bird on her back and the baby on Bird's chest, one heart bumping into the other. She'd like to sleep here, wake in falling dew. The baby holds up her head to look at Bird, to gnaw on Bird's chin, but now she's tired—spent beyond wanting and soft all at once. Everything in that baby gives way.

It is the dearest crushing feeling.

Bird makes a roll bar of her elbows and rolls with the baby against her, gently down the hill.

"Don't be afraid," she says, "like your mama. Love and be done with it. Let go. Hold on," she says, "may you always."

The baby is lying on her back, batting at Bird's face, the silver heads of the grasses nodding all around.

"I'll eat you up," Bird says, "You're too pretty. You mustn't be ashamed to be pretty. Don't be proud. People will envy you; you have to let them. People will hate you—you let them. Don't let them take anything from you, my girl. They'll take everything. You have to give yourself away."

Bird kisses the baby's pinkening cheeks, the knob of her spitty chin.

"Be good to yourself, my little lollipop. Never love a boy like Mickey. I don't mean that."

She presses her mouth against the baby's creamy belly.

"What I mean, lollipop, is love him. Love him hard and be done."

Bird picks the baby up, puts her shirt back on. The ferns are withering, sweetening the air.

"Love me," Bird says, "you have to promise. Promise me you will write to me when you are all gone away and grown."

They go inside, the kitchen dim, hard at first to see. First thing Bird sees is the telephone and she picks it up to call Mickey, hangs it up again. A grown woman. Christ above. She's got a baby. She shakes. She is shaking that baby too.

She tries Suzie. She wants to tell Suzie the sound Mickey made, the girlish, dry, collapsing gasp when he took her. But Suzie will say, "I know."

"He's got pinworms."

"Mickey?"

"My boy," Bird says.

"I'll let you go," Suzie says.

"Come on, Suzie. You don't want to know about pinworms? Quiet pale morsels you can see through, small as a grain of rice."

The pinworm eats at night, the pediatrician told Bird. "Take a look with a flashlight while he's sleeping," she advised. "They break apart as they leave the body—little fellows, friable, sliding out of the hole."

"I'm not all that wild about humans," Suzie says. "We

eat each other. We don't behave. We thought to send Mexican free-tailed bats into Japan loaded down with napalm in the second world war. Dragged them out of their caverns. Put them on ice so they'd sleep. Another shining human endeavor to rival the exploding harpoon."

Suzie takes a drag on something. Bird can hear it over the phone.

"There are too fucking many of us besides, and you and Doctor Said So just went and made two more."

"So get your tubes tied, you don't like humans," Bird says. "Be done with it."

"Right. Never give blood again."

Suzie takes another drag and a swig of something that comes in a glass with ice.

"When humans get wiped off the planet," Suzie says, "do you know this? The subways in New York City will engorge with sea water in days."

"When?" Bird says.

"What?"

"*When humans get wiped off the planet,*" Bird says. "Don't people still say *if*?"

"Matter of time," Suzie says, it's what she always says. "Maybe pinworms will do the trick. Something sneaky and easily broken. Friable, you like to say."

Bird goes back to the photo album, the bloody birth pictures, spooky, the baby still stricken and blue. Bird flips the page, going backwards, comes upon the murk that is her baby unborn, an image they make with sound.

"Here you are," Bird says, "waving. Here is the one of you sucking the pale peninsula of your thumb."

She is all spread apart, a tiny continent. A mass with migrating eyes. *Little Whale, White Moon.*

The bodies toxic. Where had Bird seen that? They were rolling belugas in cellophane, men in gloves and suits. Disposing. The whole pod—the soon-to-be-dead, the living. Beached. Bodies gasping on the strand.

You can quit the news but it finds you, some picture you didn't mean to see. That little girl dead with her books in her lap. The illuminated page. Foot soldiers, somebody's boy, creeping into the blast.

There's no way to live far enough from it. No matter the pact you make with yourself—it gets at you and eats.

Somebody's boy on the waterboard. Sounds okay to me. Says who?

Say the fat cats, says the president. *Folks, we are doing everything we can.*

Such a flocked-around helpless feeling, a rage, and Bird was chumped by it—she knew better: fat cats were making money making fear she couldn't shake. *Code orange, people, keep it calm. Now let's bump her up to code red.*

You bet. Like ants, they were, sent to scurry. Snatching for beans and Sterno, a spade. *Dig a hole. Hully up. Bring the Vizqueen.*

Sure, it passed. And when the worst of it passed you could slump back and live among the daily horrors. That was nice. The spectacle of smallpox. The war going peacably along. The icecap melted. *Owright.* The thing mutates, *owright,* but it's a frog. Heck. It's a elephant. It lives away off, it ain't you.

But it is, Bird thinks. It's you. She thinks of an old movie she saw—*mzungu* in a pith helmet stepping out of a Cessna on the vast grassy savannah, not a chance in the world to hide.

Do you say *pod*, as with whales, for the elephant? *Pod,* is it, or *tribe? A murder, a pride, a herd,* Bird thinks.

They're all out there, big as elephants, big yellow African sky.

I want that one, says the shitball, and shoots.

The animal takes a long time falling. It gives itself up in stages against its mighty will. He turns to the next elephant and takes a shot at it, too.

I want that one. And then I want that and that one then and her and her and her.

Those girls.

Columbine, pretty name, couple of quiet boys.

Those are the ones to kill you. The sheriff calls you for dental records and your life goes black and gray.

It is a day like any other, Bird thinks. Pretty place, mountains at your back, tough country. *Home. Been knowing it all my life. Lives of mine before it.*

Simple lives, used to be. Homesteaders, sheepherders.

School bus coming prettily—you can't hear it yet—up the road. You scoot her out. Not a sign, no way in the world to stop it.

But you're the mother.

You are the one who is supposed to know.

The baby hooks Bird's lip with her finger: the baby wants Bird to sing. So she sings: little snowflake, white shell, that one. And kisses all ten toes. Bird counts her lucky stars to eleven and quits. Thinks: *quit while you can and hide them, woman. The gods are greedy, too.*

She cranks the music, dances the baby upstairs. It helps. A little sunshine helps. Dewfall soon. She ought to walk back out without shoes. Pass her toes through the early glittery wet, the grass with its sparky dew.

Sparky—that's her boy's word.

Count of three. Look both ways twice.

Now move on.

Take a picture.

"Hey, hey, Mama. Take a little one of me."

"It's a little bit, it's a little bit, it's a little bit hot," her boy says.

And drops his pants from the bridge.

"Hey, take a little one of me."

What to do? Lock your babies in a closet in the dark all day and slide rice under the door? Keep them out of the sun, keep the wind from their eyes, keep them off the country road. From TV, keep them, and victorious boys, heroes hoisting the flag. From the man in a hood with the white of his palms opened skyward, wired, by head and foot and hand. From that. The next war, war to end all wars, first war of the brand new century, the unrelenting brassy gong. The poor pagans, the un- and under-chosen, the great sweeping cry to arms. To Swords! Face the Nation. From that, keep them. From the static of indecision. From desire and the absence of desire. The fly in the web that does itself in by flying. By tattered wings, by tiny dry ambitions. From that, keep them. From me, Bird thinks—goer-between, meddler. Damp consoling shade.

She could write a letter, fat chance. Scrub commodes. Here's that respite, the solitary hours—before suppertime, before the school bus comes. What to do, what to do. Try the treadmill—right.

"You'd feel better," says her husband, says Suzie.

"Better than what?" Bird says.

"You think I'm fat?" she asked her boy. "You think Mama's too fat?"

He looked her over.

"To do what?"

The baby's arms swing up, silly baby, asleep: she thinks she is falling out of a tree.

Bird washes a fork. Pays a bill and walks it to the mailbox. Comes back and picks up the phone. She won't answer, Bird thinks, but Suzie answers.

"Your poet?" Bird asks.

"Elsewhere. He went out for chips and beer."

"And he's behaving? You're okay?"

"You worry too much."

"It's a habit. It's a reason for living."

"Ah, that one," Suzie says.

"You'll see."

"Bet you five bucks I'll never."

"What?"

"You've been drinking, Bird. I hear it. You've been thinking and it isn't good. The world's done for. We've trashed the planet. There won't be water when your babies are grown."

"I can't help it."

"Sugar, you have to. Walk."

"I just did."

"Do it again. Get out. Try dancing. Make Doctor Said So keep the babies and go out and have a high time. I'll set you up, sugar. It's Italian you want, you want a Frenchman? In a heartbeat, with that hair of yours, I could find you a classy Latin. Why not? Dance a little, sugar. Let him sweat on you. Let him back you into the back of the room."

"Enough."

"Enough?" Suzie laughs. "It's almost nothing."

"I don't know why I called," Bird says.

"You're drunk, is why. And you're lonesome. You want someone to say his name to, but you won't, not even to me."

"It's easy for you. You talk to him."

"I do what I want. That's me. You're afraid to want anything. You say his name and the scenery goes to pieces. What I think? You should get in your car and find him. Leave your babies. Go to him. Find out who he still is. He's in—"

"Cut it out, Suzie Q. Don't tell me."

"Why not? He's in church next door in his underpants. He's in Ushuaia, look it up, where I saw him last, at the far away tip of the world."

"You loved him, too, don't forget."

"Fool me once," Suzie says, "many years ago."

"That worked nicely."

"Don't gloat," Suzie says. "I wanted sunshine."

"You wanted Mickey. A kitchen sink and a gingham apron. A patch of grass to mow."

"I'll let you go now, Bird. I'm going."

"You wanted to make little red-haired babies!"

"The one time and never again."

Mickey wouldn't move and then he got to moving. Bird went west with him and south, a long way around, and when they came back around to Brooklyn, Mickey looked south again. He wanted out, skip the gray.

We're soon over, said the note.

He said he was going alone. He went with Suzie.

Suzie spelled him driving south; it was winter. He had bought a car that mostly worked. His radio worked and the windows, all but one. He liked to drive in the heat with the windows down.

He would want a little place, Suzie guessed. Something. A week in a clean soft bed.

But he didn't. He had his car he thought to sleep in. He found a boat sloshed up from a hurricane he could tack a lean-to on.

"So I'm home," Suzie called Bird.

It was sleeting. Suzie needed a ride from the bus stop, she had tossed out her winter coat.

"That was useful," Bird told her, digging. "You didn't like the sun?"

Sun and wind and shadow. A boy on a swing. The grasses golden.

But the days went gray in Denver and cold and they were grounded now, evened out, and Bird's jaw had begun to stiffen. She couldn't talk much; she didn't want to.

The Drive Away clerk went north again—the forecast for old Cheyenne was windy, windy and blue.

They'd go south. South for the heat and sunshine: Nogales, Cuernavaca, La Paz. Eat peyote and sweat with the Mexicans, clear the cobwebs out.

Bird had an aunt in Albuquerque—they could stay a little while with her. She would float them a loan if they asked right and pulled her weeds in the back lot and heated her enchiladas. They'd plant hollyhocks. They would walk her dogs and pick up after them and Bird's aunt would lend them a car for a day, so Bird could show Mickey around. *That's the room I shared with my sisters, Mickey. There's the tree house. The ditch where we swam. We had horses. Here's where my rabbit is buried.*

"Hoppy?" Mickey said. "Say you're kidding."

"Why?"

"I'm making the rounds with a lunkhead who named her rabbit Hoppy? Not even Hopsalong? Not Floppy?"

He was kidding, but then he wasn't. They were in a pancake joint and he was loud.

"So what?" Bird asked.

"So what?" Mickey asked. "We nearly married. We made a baby almost. Remember? What did you think to call her?"

"Mickey, stop," Bird said, "please."

But he was started.

"You think it doesn't matter, what you name a thing?

Crazy Horse was Curly. When Crazy Horse became Crazy Horse, his father took the name Worm. You think that doesn't matter?"

He jabbed a waffle with his fork and went at the rim.

"I had an aunt named Alice, my mother's sister, I could talk to like I never talked to Mother. She had a freckle behind her ear I loved. All over, she had them all over, but that was the one I loved. She liked white food—asparagus, raspberries, cream. It was tenderer, she said, white asparagus. It made your mind clear. White food purified your thoughts. She had no children. Her skin was so white it was blue. She jumped horses. She got her foot hung up in the stirrup one day and was dragged across a field and trampled. Her skull was split. I wanted to see her. I wanted to see what her mind looked like—how clear it was, how true. Auntie Alice. My mother gave me a little pouch of her ashes. I was kid. I wet my finger and dipped it in there. White food. I ate it one flake at a time."

He dumped sugar on the table he was flicking at Bird.

"We ought to have taken what was left of her, Bird. We kept a tissue, Bird, a piece of the bloody bedsheet. Shame on me. Shame on us. We don't think right. Everything was there."

He took a breath but he wasn't finished. He took her hands in his hands. The day was darkening. It was going to get darker still.

"Bird? I'm the one who named you. Not Faith, not Hope, not Charity. Bird. There's not a bird I don't like, not exactly. I like ospreys. I like tiny owls living in holes. I like that cranes find their way by the stars while half their brain is sleeping. Mates for life. The condors that live in the Andes—those monsters mate for life, too. Geese do. Plenty of birds. It's common. They log thousands of miles, wing to wingtip. They grieve. It takes a heart of rock not to believe it. What I've read, I believe is true: you kill a condor and its mate, done in by grief, will plunge to its death from the sky. We don't believe it because we don't want to. We want to kill them ourselves with bolas. Lash them to the backs of bulls. We want to climb the trees they are sleeping in and club them on their brainy heads. Call it science. Sport. Gaucho pastime. Darwin's helpers with geology hammers. When condors sleep, they sleep hard. We call that stupid.

"Cranefly, I could have called you. I could have called you Bean. You think it matters? I called you Bird. I like birds. Birds know too fucking much, it's spooky. Your Hoppy, no doubt, was dumb. Rabbits are dumb. They die of fright. They scream. Bunny, I could have called you, but I didn't. I didn't. People should be named for themselves. You never gave me a name for anything. You call my name like everyone else. Why is that, Bird? You don't think of me? I'm Mickey like everyone else? I think you're careless, is what. You're not thinking. You're making a mark you can't see.

"Bird? If I named you for a bird I'd name you Sparrow. Maybe Wren. I thought of Phoebe, a phoebe is faithful, it comes back and goes away. Polyandrous, polyamorous, the loosely colonial—I like them all. I like chickadees, little home-body birds who stick around and sing all winter long. *Chickadee.* A bird named for its song. I like whippoorwills, sitting alone in the dark coming down. They go quiet. Then they sing the song they were named for in the dewfall and dimming woods. *Whip-poor-will.* We have to think more. We're making tracks, Bird, everybody is. There are marks where anyone has been.

"But, Bird? That baby of ours was nothing. We named her to be taken, to be nothing. She was tatters, Bird. A bloody dumpling. Think. Little Caroline, little Caroline. She was nothing. I never even wanted her. I only wanted you."

I wanted you, Bird wrote to her mother.

I'd be you.

I would wear your dresses and carry you around and in this you would be a mother again and a baby and I wouldn't be a dead baby's mother and not a girl with a dying mother, over and over again. I'd be nothing at all. I'd be you.

They were going to have to move and keep moving or else they were going down. They'd go to Albuquerque. Hitch there. It was still an idea, hitching. They would appear on the old lady's stoop in the sun and say, *It's us, hello.*

Bird bought a Styrofoam cooler for beer and twelve tall boys of Pabst. She double-bagged their clothes, brought extra bags to use as slickers—for sleet, if it came, for snow.

Her jaw was swelling; it was yellowing and blue.

They made green together, yellow and blue. Blue and red made purple.

And what did yellow and Bird make?

And what did Mickey and blue?

"And Mickey and Bird?" Mickey asked.

And Bird said, "A bloody stew."

He stuffed her hat down on her head.

"I didn't mean that," he said. "Sorry." He kissed her. "That was dumb."

"Bunnies are dumb," Bird said.

She dropped a bag at her feet and stuck her thumb out. All their clothes were lumped up in Glad bags, glisteny, thick, sturdy things slouched on the snowy berm.

"I'll call you Man Afraid," Bird said. "Sleeps A Lot. Sound good?"

She could talk still so she was talking. Pretty soon, she would quit.

What they had come to see, they had seen by then: the salt pillars, the burying grounds. The concrete Garden of

Eden—ugly, ugly, that kook in his cut-away coffin on perpetual display. They took pictures: meals they had eaten, neon signs, Mickey's boots tipped over in the road. They took a ten-second film of a pear they ate, the pear stood up on a fencepost with a bite taken out, another bite, as with time lapse, until it was a slumping core.

This then this then this: days hooked together like poptops in a lacerating chain.

They hauled their cooler off into the bushes and lined out a last line of junk. A little boost. They were going to miss that: the tidy gray packets that Mickey kept with the bloody scrap of bedsheet they saved, with Maggie's dewclaw and a daisy and the curl of a Hasidim boy.

They waited together in the bushes until they had both thrown up. Disgusting—throwing up with your jaw clamped shut. They washed out their mouths with beer.

They had left their Glad bags on the shoulder in the snow and somebody stopped, a big guy, slow, and threw them into the back of his wagon. He drove a wood-paneled wagon from the 70s, the last of its lovely kind. Government man. If it was on the shoulder, he picked it up. That was the job the state paid him to do.

They could smell the wagon before they reached it—acrid, ammoniac—but their clothes were already in back. The storm was picking up and the cloud socked in and snow had seeped into their bootsoles. They got in.

Mickey tried breathing through a sack of orange peels: that helped. Bird let her head swing down between her knees. There were bodies in back, road kill, a sticky heap, legs and legs, the mess of death and weather.

Bird saw a match on the floorboard and lit it and her tooth ignited, hideous lump, and the nectar she had tasted since Kansas bubbled up at the root of her tongue. She swung her head up and reached for the door of the car.

"Get me out."

They got out, ferried as far as the second ramp south without their first citation.

"How you feel?" Mickey said.

"Pretty drifty. Nice."

"Wish we had more of it."

"Good thing we have you."

"I'd like the Hyatt. A hot bath."

"So nice," Bird said.

"The lights at our feet of the city."

"Yeah. Pizza Hut delivered."

"I'm not hungry."

"Neither am I. I may never be hungry again."

They tossed snowballs at passing traffic.

"We'll cause an accident."

"We *are* an accident."

"You don't believe that."

"I don't, it's true."

They tried hitching for a time with Mickey hidden in the brush that poked out over the driftings of snow, a new tactic: the lone female, the vagrant waif.

No dice. There was Bird's jaw puffed up, pooched along the toothbone—blue, bruised, her mouth lumped shut.

Somebody fishtailed an El Camino, flipped her off, sent a gray dollop of slush to break against her neck. A boy leaned from his window, screaming, "I AM SCREAMING AT YOU!" and sped south, south to cactus and sage and piñon and sun, the curve of Bird's clean horizon. Lizards in the woodpile. Frizzy-headed seeds of cottonwood, soup of the Rio Grande. Old home.

I'd like to get there, Bird thought.

They would never get there. They would piddle days away on the interstate, on the off-ramp, on the on.

She thought of an old song and sang it: the one about the bicycle, the roller skate, the key.

"Hello, love," Mickey said, and goosed her.

He had come up out of hiding to her, creeping through the brush.

"I missed you."

I miss Maggie, Bird thought.

"I miss Maggie," Mickey said. "If she were here, she would take down your hair."

He took her hair down and worked his fingers through it.

He chewed up a grape for Bird for a poultice, something to draw the heat. Every hour Bird's tooth felt hotter, and the skin of her cheekbone sparkled, how it felt. By and by she couldn't open her mouth more than the width of his tongue, should he wish, and he wished it, and moved to kiss her, her face blazing and plumped and solid, tight, and Bird lost for an instant the difference again—between what was hers, what his. His tongue was briefly cool in the heat of her mouth and then like something liquid, warmed, melted away, that she was free to swallow.

Free and clear, free and clear, how Bird tells it.

"You were broke," Suzie says, "and cold."

"We ate our meals off a bucket."

"Meaning what?" Suzie asks.

"Didn't matter."

"It would matter to you now," Suzie says.

"I'm not saying. We were kids. It's all different."

"You're who's different, sugar. I haven't changed."

"We were happy," Bird insists.

"You were high. It's nice. Get happy, get high. Have a party in your pants. It doesn't last," Suzie says. "It's not supposed to."

Mickey sat on a Glad bag beside her. Bird was cold and would cry if he touched her.

And so he touched her.

"It's not your fault," Bird said.

He knew it was: whatever it was she was thinking.

He turned the ring on her finger, the ruby her mother wore.

"We could pawn it," he suggested, and wished he hadn't.

He wished he were rich and quick on his feet and brave enough to lie down and close his eyes.

"What else?" Bird wondered.

"Taller. A pilot. A poet. And better to you."

She would be finished soon, crying. If he kissed her, she would cry some more.

A dog lunged from the back of a pickup truck to get at them, and the sound drove a spike through Bird's head.

"Fucking dog," Mickey shouted, and ran after it.

A glove fluttered up on the highway in the wind of whatever was passing, a whole forest borne south on flatbeds, double-wides and I-beams, a donkey once, out in the wind, with its great swiveling ears.

America. America.

The reel was dizzying—the cattle trucks with their bellowing mobs, the soon-to-be-dead, the living, the vast flotilla of family vans, kiddos hooked up to laptops, DVDs, junkies, mavens, shit for brains.

Fuzzed out.

Made sense to them: you fuzz out. Sink in. Out of the clamorous world.

Bird lay her head in Mickey's lap. She could feel her heart beat in her mouth and the rock she had given him in his pocket. It was a smooth, dark rock, rounded and cool they traded as they traveled.

"I wish I could make you happy, Bird."

"I'll be happy."

He slid a bracelet he had woven from brittle grass onto Bird's wrist and kissed her.

"For the next two hundred years."

"Toss it," Suzie says. "You keep too much. You hoard."

Bottle caps and matchbooks. Tooth in a box. A bracelet of grass. The little dry stem of that pear.

Too little, too much, next to nothing.

Whitened bone and sucking rock, the acorn when her water broke, Baby's first booger, Baby's gilded shoe.

Bird carries the bloodied tissue still, slipped into a see-through plastic sleeve in her wallet where pictures go— where they would go if she could remember, or if she were a better mother, or if she weren't so superstitious, or soft-hearted, or hard.

She gets her birth dreams back, belated. Births an enormous zucchini the doctor comes at with a knife: *You don't want to watch this.*

Dreams the baby is plastered into the wall.

"Hiya," says the baby at daybreak and by nightfall, the balm of dark, says, "Hiya hiya hiya yeah yeah yeah."

The day's fresh trick—going, gone.

Memorable, forgotten.

Bird wakes with her boy, with the rope of cold rolled out along her spine and thinks: *Were you not, my goose, smaller by far when I last lay down with you? Before you let me have a sniff at you? Before I rose and shut the door?*

They lie awake together, his soft boy-toes cramped and curled at the foot of his footed pajamas. They are watching the last green artifice of stars shrinking on his ceiling.

Pfft!

Growing, grown, unguarded in sleep. Oh, Mama.

She does the math, the years to come, the school bus whistling down the hill, small pale jostled faces. She sees a girl, another's, braids undone, flyaway standing-up hair—that's her face. It's Bird's face. The girl of herself, the little, she thinks—

And turns away and thinks: *Mickey.*

Never can see the man coming.

Bird laughs to herself to think of it, *coming, I'm coming,* remembers Tuk and Doll Doll, the pair who picked them up, the pair they took a room with, briefly, finally, in the blowing heat of a roadside hotel, remembers Tuk going at it, mama-talking Doll Doll, snuffling around in her culotte, whistling through his nose.

Back again: a speeding reel. Back in the honeyed swim and slop, a roving, animal hunger. Just a nibble.

Not a nibble, not enough, not near.

Bird got behind herself and bit Mickey, dug into him with a fork. The moment's impulse.

The body food.

Her girl blue from the womb, dead, Bird thought: *I'll have to eat her. Want me just to eat you?*

She remembers Tuk slurping at her—not her, not Bird—at Doll Doll, Bird waking up from a dream of herself in the velvety dark of the room they shared and in it was somebody slurping pudding from a bowl like a dog. Eat you out.

Eat you in, Bird thought—that was more like it. And having waked, she slept, and having slept, waked, and waking again heard the tidal shush of skin on skin, coming, going, *Mama now, I'm coming, Mama,* Tuk hollering, a drawn-out *o, coooming, rwaorwaorwaor,* and then he barked it out: *I went! I went! I went!*

"He wore a shirt that read *Big Boys Hold It*," Bird says.

"That's stupid," Suzie says.

"Bunnies are stupid," Bird says.

"What was your name before your name was Bird?"

"I forget."

"No you don't, sugar. You know ravens—"

"Yes. Juggle sticks in the air."

"For fun," Suzie says, "for the fuck of it."

"And lie in ants with their wings spread open," Bird adds.

"For the fuck of it. For the feeling. Ecstasy and nothing more."

They went up, up some more.

"Half a mile above the mile-high city," Mickey said, "not too shabby."

They would spend the last of their high at the Hyatt, why not? He had a credit card he'd swiped from his mother she didn't yet know was gone.

They were in a steaming bath with bubbles to their chins when Bird said, as her mother used to say, "Wonder what the poor folks are doing."

"This," Mickey said, and lifted Bird by her ass to his mouth in the froth and pushed into her with his tongue.

"Home again," he murmured. "Hallelujah."

They wore their Hyatt robes, heavy as hides; they smelled of lavender and money.

They ate prime rib, bloody rare, and a heap of mashed potatoes; drizzled-on food and reductions, a feast, a bottle of wine.

What if they ate like this once a week like wolves, fattening and fasting, running lean, gorging themselves again?

"What if I touched you here," Mickey said, and slid

his hand between her legs beneath the table, "and nowhere else, ever again?"

The robe they took and the embellished towel took up half the room in their Glad bags and made a softer place to sit. Bird was tender still, seepy.

They sat around a lot, they stood. They tried the off-ramp and the on.

Three days—they'd made maybe a hundred miles. Too high, this country, the clouds snow-gray, too close to their heads. Unbudged.

Somebody slowed down, stopped, backed up, peeled out. Very funny.

Bird's tooth throbbed in her head.

They went back to throwing snowballs into traffic to pass the time. Drank a Pabst, split it, split the next. And the beer and being in the cold all day and the heat of Mickey's breath when he kissed her made everything floaty and bright. The brightness, the float; the beat skipped, a hitch—Mickey felt it too. The blessed looseness of slipping out of time.

They quit bothering to stick their thumbs out, quit bothering to stand but to fish another beer from the cooler where they sat.

She heard her name, spoke it, understood that she had spoken it meaning to speak to him.

Said to Mickey, "Hey, Bird?"

Remember that?

It had begun to snow again, the slow fat flakes suspended. They sat quietly, didn't move.

As at auction.

Took a sip.

As the old, didn't move.

Wanted nothing.

The mind swept. The smallest act. A name spoken. How the heart—this was the real heartache: this happiness: this lonely, buzzing elation.

Can't last.

Couldn't last. Nature of things.

Somebody quick say why.

Wanting so mostly rarely withstands the presence of the thing we want.

Say why.

A ride, for instance. The golden Ryder. Which arrives when we are flagging, pleased, happy without it, why?

Why—having traveled for days to reach someplace—are we nonetheless unready to stand up and walk through the door?

Hello, hello.

Not yet a little.

They sat their cooler. Forgetful. Forgetting.

The Ryder rocked to a stop on the shoulder.

Last time.

One more last time, says her boy.

And so they sat some. They stood to meet it.

There were two of each, human and dog, the pups part wolf—one was Wolfie, the other fluffed and white. This was Snowball.

"I'm Bird," Bird said, "and this is Mickey," and of the two it was Tuk who spoke and said, "I expect you are."

He was dressed like a man of the region weathered into his middle years—in a worked-over hat, a bandanna at the neck. Doll Doll was a kid in pantyhose, in a bodysuit like bubble wrap, her culotte a bilious plaid. She had a candy necklace between her teeth she was sucking the color from. The dye left a smeary chinstrap of many muddied colors.

She made herself small when Bird and Mickey got in, scooted over in the truck against Tuk. Tuk licked her, and licked her some more, Doll Doll offering him her neck. She had her sleeves pulled down and over her hands after the fashion of girls of the season. She brought a sleeve to her mouth and sucked at it. It was wet all the way to the elbow.

The pups were loose in the cab of the truck and Doll Doll's pantyhose was pinked with blood where the pups had

gotten at her in the wide miles since Cheyenne. Tuk swung
the truck into traffic and tumbled the pups across the floorboards—over Doll Doll's feet and Mickey's and Bird's, a
tidy row, tightly packed across the bench seat—like a seat
on a bus, mottled and split, vinyl, a school bus smell. When
Doll Doll bent to reach for a pup they all had to lean and
twist away.

Doll Doll let Wolfie walk across her lap to Mickey's open hands. He tucked the pup under his jacket and
scratched her behind her ear: this set her paw to thumping. Wolfie wrinkled her face and drooled, shaking with
puppy bliss.

"You got her spot," Doll Doll said. "Oh, Wolfie."

Doll Doll reached across Bird to lay her hand on the
pup snugged into Mickey's jacket. Bird leaned out lightly
against Doll Doll's arm, her long dampened sleeve pulled
longer, the crepey violet bubbles of Doll Doll's bodysuit col-
lapsed. Doll Doll moved away not at all. She had her arm set
stiff across Bird's chest: a reminder, a locking bar: here she
was. Bird was going to be where she had put herself, now and
again, decided or not: she got the kid-at-a-county-fair feeling she gets: feels the heat and wild sickening swing of what
she wants, has picked and paid for, thought she wanted: rag-
dolled, the snapping plunge, the quieting climb before you
fall so fast you are lifted up and floating.

She was floating: that was love.

Love did away with the instant between wanting and doing, wanting to kiss and kissing, wanting to bite and biting—and so Bird bit the girl hard on the arm through the cheap rough crepe she was wearing.

"Hey! You can't—Tuk, she—"

"You can't bite her," Tuk said. "Now you'll have to—"

"You have to say you're sorry," Doll Doll said. "And I'll say I forgive you."

But she wasn't: Bird was saving *sorry* up for children, a husband, a demoted family dog. For the months to come, the hand through the wall, Mickey's tender wrists he opened. The little closures and retreats.

"So how do you like God's country?" Tuk wanted to know.

Bird mumbled a mousy answer; her jaw felt soldered shut. The fat of her cheek and sinew, the woofer and tube of her ear, the pores, how it felt, sizzled; anvil and hammer and stirrup; ampulla and tragus, inward and out: nimble, any lasting pain, referred to neighbors, the wagging tongue; to the puffy glistening tab of her throat, to gingiva and palate, the string and ocherous wax of her eyes: hot, all of it, sparkling, every living cell: septum, foramen, cementum; the horn of pulp and the chamber—the tooth jigsawed into tissue, into alveolar bone. The whole bright box of Bird's head hurt.

She had taken to biting strangers.

She had gotten what she deserved.

Mickey was wearing his shirt sprung at the neck and Bird could see the upmost clusters she loved of freckles on his chest. She couldn't stand it: Doll Doll had them too. They had like bodies, long and light for distance, the miles across the plain.

Bird mouthed it: *I want out. I want you.*

A suite with a theme, Bird wanted, something jungly, sneaky, scrawk and howl, a costume, the purr of rain, a bed set lazily spinning among the ravenous trees. She wanted Mickey to tie her by her hands and feet and work her slowly open. Make her cry out. Make her bleed.

A tableau, she wanted. But not this one.

Tuk was hooking snot from his nose with his long little fingernail, just the one long one, all he needed, and rolling it into a ball. He cracked the window, flicked the ball into the airstream. Hooked the next wet glob he rolled dry.

It was warm in the truck and dewy and nice and nice to be out of the cold. And they were going where they meant to be going. Going south to Albakuke. Be there in a day.

Bird moved away not to touch Mickey, to be some away from the heat of him and the drug of the way he smelled. She set her mind on Doll Doll—on the smeary mess she had made of her chin, on Doll Doll's atrocious clothes. She had swiped her eyelids with blue glitter. A kid. A doll! and new to things.

She was trying to look Bird's age, Bird thought, and failing. That helped. And the little round hump of her belly helped: ah ha, a flaw, Doll Doll long and light, but soft, too—weak, Bird thought.

But the next thought was creeping in: *Is that a baby in your belly?*

Which it was.

Two discs of red appeared between Doll Doll's knees where her knees fell helplessly together. Doll Doll would come to limp and ache, Bird thought, comforted. She would age into polymer sockets, the daily complaints of living.

Bird leaned to kiss him. There was nothing she wouldn't do for Mickey, now and now and ever.

But he was talking. He was missing his dog.

"We had a dog once," he said. "She was Maggie. She liked to take down Bird's hair."

"It's so pretty, your hair," Doll Doll told her, and touched the ends to her lips as if to eat it.

"She slept for heat between me and Bird with her back to me and her legs out. She stuck all four of her legs out, stiff, like this, to keep Bird off me. She used to chew Bird's toothbrush up and stash the leftover bits of her shoes and the cast-off strands of her dental floss (*and the vomited wads of tampons,* Bird thinks) underneath my pillow."

"She found an old coat," Bird offered, "to sleep on and she slept with it over her head."

"Oh, Maggie," Doll Doll said.

"You all stop now," Tuk said. "You'll make her weepy.

She's got that—syndrome, stray—whatever you call it. She's tender and you'll make her sad."

"I'm not sad," Doll Doll said.

"Well, you will be. Think a moment of your mule, of your turtle, back to home. Your maimed and crippled. Think of a moment of Bim and Toto, near drowned, of your colicky armadillo. The calf born without any eyeballs."

"The Chinese farmer who grew three tongues," Mickey offered. "He could lick the one with two others. He could reach back and lick his ears. Think of that."

Mickey fluttered his tongue at Bird and Doll Doll turned in time to see it.

"Yuck," Doll Doll said, which was a comfort.

Yuckity lickity schmuckity fuck. Keep your feet in a bucket. Keep your head.

"We got too many to care for," Tuk told her, and twanged her necklace against her chin.

"We got some acres," he admitted. "A dab of a place down to Texas. A creek with a pawky flow. Bit of grass. Bunchgrass, cheet. Whatever. Feed. I drove a stake in the dust to hitch the goat down to. Round and round he goes."

"It's nice," Doll Doll said. "It's home and it's dry and quiet. You can hear the beer fizz in your bottle. Sky. Wide dry blue eye quiet. And the yellow grasses move. And Tuk? We got that one cottonwood tree for shade I will never again shade under."

"Now, Doll."

"You know I won't."

"I heard that."

"I brought this cat home," Doll Doll offered.

"I wish you wouldn't."

"He's ashamed. He don't want it told."

"That cat—"

"I know it. Needed helping. He needed helping bad. Such as I did, Tuk. You remember? I was eating out of a bowl."

"I do. And I remember that old tom popping. It spit. Ringwormy, rabid, god knows. How he howled among the leaves in the shadows, peering down."

"'Get him down,' you said, 'or I'll shoot him!'"

"Little Bit, it is nothing I ever wished to do."

They went along some, quiet, Doll Doll sucking at her sleeve. The clouds ate away at the mountains. You couldn't see much.

"I can't see."

She banged her head on the dashboard. She was blacking out, holding her breath, "I can't see."

"Now, Doll?"

"I fucking hate these fucking mountains and these fucking wasted trees."

Tuk swung the truck onto the shoulder and held her.

"Talk it out," he whispered. He stuffed his fingers in her ears. "Use your words."

Doll Doll hummed and sniffled and Tuk kissed a patch on the top of her head where the hair had been snatched out. He closed his eyes.

Forgot, or seemed to, that they were not alone. Wind rocked the truck. Snowball whimpered and yipped. The heat was off and the cold seeped in and the steam they all made on the windows frosted prettily to ice.

"Take your breath," Tuk instructed, and tipped her chin up so Mickey and Bird could see.

Doll Doll was smiling again, trying to.

"Now make these poor people feel at home."

The sun smudged through the clouds as if on cue and all their faces pinked up but for Doll Doll's, which was smeared a gluey blue.

"What a day, what a day for driving," Tuk declared.

"I go for the suffering dumb."

"If you smack a fly—" Tuk said.

"Eat it. You have to eat anything you run over or otherwise maim or kill. It's a rule. So you won't. While we travel."

"Friends, it isn't only you. She'll tug a frog, for instance, from the mouth of a snake. She'll bring a spider in from the cold. She poured sugar out in the kitchen for the ants—*they have to eat, too.* Freed an ox from its traces, a honeybee from a web. She lets the cows out—"

"—to run with the dogs—" Doll Doll said.

"—and with the llama she's set loose and the chickens.

Plus the shoat! the open range! a 900-pound pig! Gone off to grub every posey patch, every hillock of beans in the county."

"I do do that. It's my nature," Doll Doll said. "I have a very free and helpful nature. I like a gate that's open. I like Wolfie here and Snowball and how we all light out together like this and let each other go."

"Gather up, giddyup. Take a picture. Make it quick! A hard little sprint and she'll be gone."

"I'm very Doll Doll," Doll Doll admitted. "I'm very moving on."

Tuk shook his head agreeably—an agreeable man, easy to love, in a hapless sort of way. Surprised by himself—that was the feeling. He clouded over at a clap and his hands shook and he shored himself up against the steering wheel to steady himself to say, "So who is it cleans up after? Tuk baby cleans up after. That's Doll Doll all the way."

"After what?" Doll Doll said.

"Whatever you're finished with. Anything gimpy or little, try. Try the lonely. What's weary, what's maimed."

He pulled his hat up, which tweaked his eyebrows. He looked more surprised than ever.

"Ever living one."

"Ever living what?" Doll Doll said.

"Ever. Living. One."

"She's not," Bird said, "living."

"She?"

"Maggie," Bird said. "You know, the dog?"

"Is your mama?"

"What?"

"Living. Dead? Is she dead?" Doll Doll asked, hopefully.

"She—" but Bird had never said it out among strangers in the world.

"Or your daddy either one are they—"

"Living?"

"Have you got any people anywhere she wants to know still living?" Tuk explained. "Because her mama is dead and her papa. Her sister is dead and her brother. And her sister's little girl who was just a little girl and the fish and the rabbit and the dog. All her dolls burned up and her dresses and shoes and any little person or treasure that was hers and her hairbrush and matching mirror set with the handles inlaid with jewels. Flamed up. She was in the yard out watching. She was not supposed to be in the yard at all. She was supposed to be up high where her people lived, doing the morning chores."

"It was a little dry yard fenced around," Doll Doll added, "how my mama wanted. So nobody could snatch me. Mama put up a high fence, singing. She sang songs from the church and the country while she worked and weaved the fence with flowers. They were flowers you could find in the desert. You could maybe find them here."

"If you looked," Tuk said, "if you were lucky. But you're not lucky, sugar lump. You never have been."

"Tuk wants to take me back there to look at it. I don't want to, I never will."

"A body runs and runs," Tuk said. "Nobody gets away. People don't think, they're in a hurry. It isn't small. They park the car, can't think, can't be bothered. City folks, big city life, too much on their minds. Park double. Save a sec. Park anywhere, park triple. Suit yourself, okey doke, move along. Make a deal! Barking on your cellaphone. Flashers in the fire lane. Hope for the best, move on. Fire trucks can't move? Kids and babies? Okey doke. Back in a flash, back in two, hope for the best, hey Johnny? Lord. They'd be alive today, your people, if not for that fellow in a hurry parked so the fire trucks couldn't move. It's the truth. Show your arms, sugar lump, they're like plastic. Melted down. And you're the one got away. Just a kid, hanging on the chain link, watching. Just a kid how you see left living, call it living. I found her laid out in the Greyhound station in Waxahatchie, Texas. She had a little blanket she slept on. She was eating out of a bowl."

Doll Doll had pulled up her knees to her chest and stretched her bodysuit down across them, unsnapped. The crepe made a tent to her ankles, a hole big enough at the collar to stick down her face down through.

"I found you sleeping, Little Bit. You had your thumb in your mouth. When I picked you up and carried you you never once opened your eyes or moved all the way I carried you home."

"You called it home," Suzie says, "but it was slumming. It was dumb. You could have lived uptown where I live. You could have moved to that beloved country where you holed up the week in that wind you both liked. That is Prairie Lee's wind. It always was, Bird. You can't have it. You never really could."

"Now we have heard from one small country."

"Be nice," Suzie says. "You thought he'd marry, that was hard. Now it's hard he never did. What is that? You're not happy? You don't want to live how you do?"

"But I do," Bird says.

"Exactly."

"I want to stay right here," Bird says. "It's quiet and I like the seasons and how it all moves out and in. It's like rooms outside when the leaves come and every road's a tunnel and everything's moving in. It closes in. I've learned to like that."

"You know why?" Suzie says. "Because it's autumn. The leaves are falling. The woods open up. Anytime things are moving out, you're in love with moving in."

"You might be right," Bird says.

"Trust me. You say it every spring and every fall. That's not your place, Bird. I don't know what is. The great dry blue-eyed quiet? Could be. But when's the last time you saw it, sugar? How long has it been?"

Bird wrote: *I saw the old place, Mother.*

It was all hemmed in by houses. The ditch where the red mare threw you dried up and they filled it in. They tore the barn down. Didn't need it, I guess. The little cross is still there for Hoppy in the mint we planted for our drinks that day. Did I want to come in? the people asked me.

I said, "Here is where my daddy backed his truck over my bike. Here is where he rolled off the rooftop from being up there on his crutches."

The hollyhocks were blooming.

"We had horses," I told them, "we had geese."

Now we don't. My kids are growing up without them. That's all right, I guess. I don't know.

I never went inside. I'm glad I didn't. I don't guess I ever will.

"Guess how old I am," Doll Doll said.

"Twenty?" Bird guessed as a courtesy.

Doll Doll was seventeen.

"Guess what music I like."

"Country?"

"Country, sure, but who?"

"Johnny Cash?"

"Naw."

"Merle Haggard?"

"Guess another couple of times."

Bird had one more name she could think of and it wasn't Patsy Cline. It was Patsy Cline who Doll Doll loved.

"I had all of her. Ever song she ever sung. I had alligator boots like Patsy's, a gift to me from a boy named Hank."

"Hank was vermin," Tuk said.

"Was not."

"A bona-fide life-sucker."

Doll Doll pulled out a snapshot to show them: Hank and his souped-up Trans Am, a girl tossed against the hood with her blouse half off.

"That's you?" Mickey asked.

"It isn't. But don't you just love that car? Baby blue. Slant six. Seats of leather."

"Sure."

"That car was soon to be mine. Hank swore it."

"Hank swore plenty," Tuk said.

"Swore he'd kill you," Doll Doll said.

"But he didn't."

"Nope. Which is why we have come to be here."

"You're moving?" Mickey asked.

"We're from Texas," Doll Doll said. "It's big country. Big sky and a good slab of brisket. Baby blue Trans Am. You light out. Ride around, look at the country."

She bit a disc of candy from her necklace that colored her lips and tongue.

"I like every sort of a road," Doll Doll said, "like dirt how it rolls up behind you, the oil road, I like the smell of it. Rain! Like when it's dry in summer and a cloud darkens up you can see away off in the basin. Maybe you have got the top down. You are driving so fast to get there. You don't know are you going to get there before the rain quits or what. But you do! You've got the top down. You put your face up. Up! The rain's like needles. And you are flying, you are flying all the way through. Then *waaaa*. You're out and the rain is behind you. It's just sun and heat and the smell of it and the blacktop is fucking steaming bright and you can scarcely breathe. Right? Do you know, Tuk? You can't breathe right. And the cloud is lifting up with the rain hanging down and sliding off and there's a shadow. And the shadow is like the sea. I haven't even ever been to the sea. I haven't been to Galveston."

"Where the girls walk into the water with confetti in their hair," Tuk said, like somebody quoting something. "I can take you there, I will, Little Bit. Sit out on a towel beside the sea."

He slipped his hand in under her culotte. He had scratched a hole in her pantyhose and laid the weight of one finger there.

"How long you been driving?" Mickey asked.

"Months. Maybe six."

"He knocked me up in the back back there. We got a bedroll in back with the peanuts where we flop most every night."

"You sleep in the truck?"

"We do. With the peanuts. Patsy Cline on the radio. Works out all around."

Tuk said, "Sunshine, best little nut. Cooler full of beer and tapato chips."

"It's real nice," Doll Doll said. "Bit of quiet. The pups in front. It's what we need."

They had come into surplus peanuts, nearly half a ton of them in 40-pound mesh bags. An idea Tuk had. It would pay for the trip—they went from See's to See's. By day, they delivered peanuts. They hauled the mesh bags off the mattress at night and heaped them up on all sides. They lay down together in the clearing they had made—shored up, sandbagged in, a thumb stuck in the dike against doom.

"Ever penny we make, we spend it," Doll Doll said. "Food, petroleum, beer. It's time we got back to Texas."

"Time for brisket."

"It is. I haven't eaten," Doll Doll said, "I've been dizzy. Supposably I eat for two but who in the world can do that? I can't eat. I hardly sleep. I keep dreaming. I dreamed I swallowed a wasp and died."

"You're homesick, is all. You miss your animals."

"I dreamed Hank killed ever one of them. Ever. Living. One."

"Quit, sunshine. It's just you're blurry."

"There is too much of something in me—I can scarcely think or see."

Doll Doll dropped her face into the tent her bodysuit made when it was stretched over her bent legs.

"That Hank is a waste of clothes," Tuk confided.

"Hey!" She looked up. "Something happened! Something in me moved."

Doll Doll stretched the elastic band of her culotte out to look at the hummock where the baby was. All they saw at first was Doll Doll's heart bumping in her stomach.

"Hey, nugget," she said. "Everybody all at once say nugget."

It was a very obedient nugget and took a tumble in the sack on cue.

She snapped her culotte back.

"That is just too weird."

Mickey looked at Bird. She'd gone missing.

He leaned into her and whispered, "Everything is yours."

By then Tuk had pulled the truck over and come back up the bank with a loaf of bread.

"It's froze," he explained, "might be good still."

They sat in the truck and watched him with the heat still blowing hard. Tuk was gathering rocks, searching for a flat spot on a rock to stack on the flat of another.

He meant to mark the trail: *here they were when.*

First proof of the life to be.

Doll Doll jabbed at the horn, sulky. How like a man—out

building a shaky totem to mark the somersault of a plum. Plum, bunny, nugget. The least unsmoothened sandy ball in the bearings of the planet would bring it down. A cricket would tip it, a southbound finch.

When he had finished, Tuk motioned to them and Bird and Mickey dropped out of the truck, looking back to Doll Doll, Doll Doll mouthing, "Not me, I'm cold."

Dusk had seeped into the land by then and from the ground grew the lifting blue of night, a shade rising, and the day-wind stilled. Cold made the wet air heavy. The dome light was on in the cab of the truck, a buttery, come-to-me yellow, and the truck was gliding away.

"There goes Doll Doll," Tuk said. "She won't go far. She'll drive off the ramp to the Chevron and ask to use the phone. Call the cops to haul me off. I knock her around, she'll tell them. Well, I'd like to. Times as these, I'd like to. She likes a scene, is all. We'll get through it," he said. "Adios, nugget."

"Adios, nugget," Mickey chimed in, and the three of them walked down the road.

Tuk was right: there was a scene and they got through it.

Bird and Mickey stayed in the truck. Mickey drove the truck around to where the dumpsters sat beside golden limber willows and a frozen pond. They heard coyotes, their high wild mourning song. He had the doors locked, Bird's jeans at her knees.

"Love you up," Mickey said, and gingerly, mostly quietly, it was done.

They buttoned up when they spotted Doll Doll in the fish-eye round of the side view mirror. She tossed herself at the door.

"We thought something happened. Or worse," she said.

"We been all over this country this side of the Great Divide," Tuk said, getting in, "and I never saw a soul so ugly as that one. I wish you wouldn't—"

"I'm sorry," Doll Doll said.

"And I forgive you."

They still had one See's to get to and it was close to closing time. Doll Doll read directions and they turned off the ramp going west.

"Remember that creep who had tattoos of flies crawling all over his neck?"

"Where was that at?" Tuk couldn't remember.

"South Dakota," Doll Doll said.

She was the navigator. She knew the nicknames of all fifty states: Land of Enchantment; the Show-Me State; Beehive; Cornhusker; Tar Heel; Sooner. *Manly Deeds, Womanly Words; To the Stars through Difficulties. If You Seek a Pleasant Peninsula, Look about You. She Flies with Her Own Wings.*

"We saw Indians," Doll Doll said. "We saw a cross a thousand feet tall."

"In a bean field?" Bird asked.

"That's the one. Go right. Go right right here on Petaluma, Tuk."

Tuk took a right on Straw.

"Shit," Doll Doll said, "you're a slow leak."

"I saw a donkey in the bed of a pickup truck," Bird said.

"Yuh huh," Doll Doll said, "I like to see that."

"And a kid with a pup and a Hoola Hoop. And the roadside marker where Clara died—with a wreath and a tin can of flowers at the foot and a life-sized blow-up doll. Did you see that?" Bird asked, mumbled, wanted to spit but could not.

"I need a napkin," Bird said.

"Not mine," Doll Doll said. "Mine's got all the directions. Three lights, turn south, bear left, go west. We got to get back to Petaluma."

"Hold your horses, Little Bit."

Doll Doll didn't like it—the start and stop, too much to see, a racket. She liked a little town to sail through. A kid mowing grass in her underpants. Old boys sipping sody, sipping sody, eating beans.

"You got kids, guys? Got a kitten?" Tuk asked. "Any little thing to look after—to get your minds off yourselves? Them little turtles? You got a cellaphone? I need to make a call."

Doll Doll pouted and glowed.

"I'm just talking, Little Bit."

Tuk stuck out his tongue and made a ditch of it he sucked spit loudly through.

"She wants a cellaphone," he explained. "There's a color of green and yellow she wants with sort of crumbs of gold. For the baby, for when the baby is ready to come out, which is pretty soon, pretty soon. We got a wind-her-up thing for it to look at."

"It's like nothing, Tuk. Like we made it up. It used to not even move."

"It'll move," Tuk said. "Get the hiccumups, keep you awake till dawn."

"Is it a girl?" Bird asked.

"How should he know?"

"I know several things," Tuk said.

"Well, you don't know Straw from Petaluma, I guess. Now take another right right here."

He did. Next was a left on Pisgah that Tuk sailed right on through.

"I don't get it," Doll Doll said. "I said Pisgah. Then comes Aspen and Birch and Catalpa, like the alphabet, right in a row. He's been doing this since Texas!"

She was banging her head on the dashboard again.

"It plain escapes me. I say Poplar he turns on Pisgah, left on Oak he takes Willow, it's like—" but Doll Doll fell short of a likeness and covered her face with her hands.

Tuk turned the truck around and missed the turn and turned it around again. Tumbled the pups across the floorboards, drove at last past See's.

"See's See's See's! Can't you read?" Doll Doll bellowed. "Can't you read, Tuk?"

And then it struck her.

She was quiet. Mickey and Bird were quiet. The pups quit gnawing on Tuk's bootsoles and sat on their tails and drooled.

"I do believe you cannot read, Tuk."

There he was: a man squeezed into a truck with strangers, with a girl he had picked up eating from a bowl on the floor of the Greyhound station. He had thrown out her makeup kit. She was nearly too pretty without it to be seen with a cowpoke like him. Pokey boy. Never took to school. Poked the teacher with a stick in the privy. That boy, not a bad boy, good with numbers. Not a man much for words. He had mostly learned to get along without them and without people much or much in the way of tables and chairs and fresh new shirts with pearly snaps and their arms pinned back in plastic. He liked the smell of dust and sage. He liked a suitcase fine to eat his food from, a rag for a tablecloth. Pabst in cans: good enough. That was living—the rash spare days people boasted of once they'd lived a safe stretch out past them.

Poor. Fine by him.

Ignoramus. Well, it hurt. Made him mean.

What to do?

He'd give her pups away. He'd smash a schoolboy's bike with the Ryder. Stuff his pockets with lollipops. Cheat and snitch and scream. That'd help.

"This is where you get out," he said. "Out. O-U-T."

Ha, spelled it. Let her chew on that.

Tuk opened a can of beer and guzzled it. Dropped the empty for the pups to cut their gums on—her pups. How about that?

"Howcome you never did tell me, Tuk? Now supposably we have got this baby coming and what are we going to do?"

He worked his tongue in his mouth.

"Oh, Tuk," Doll Doll said.

Street signs, simple signs—what? He figured she would do it for him, him a grown man?

Tuk dropped his head onto the steering wheel, rammed the truck into a Sani-Hut, threw up in the ashtray and cried.

"Well, it's a story," Suzie says.

"You always say that. *Something to pass the time.*"

"They were misfits," Suzie says. "You never saw them again. They were like you some way you can't name."

"Maybe that."

"Gypsies. Looking for something to care for. Something to feed and flee."

"Now we have heard from one—"

"—small country. Or else you're making it up."

"Making what up?"

"Your mother club. Your marriage. Your plain quiet shut-away life. It's not enough but you can't let on. So you tell yourself loopy stories about people you can't love or be. The tragically illiterate. The orphan with a fluffy puppy and a get-away Trans Am. Dog people. Dogs are so people feel forgiven. Lock a dog in the cellar to starve and it shatters to happy pieces to see you again. I never wanted that. Not even a cat, even as a kid, cats are for the sad and lonely. Bossy melanchol-ics. Give me a mouse or a turtle: it will never know I'm gone."

"I drowned a pink-eyed mouse by accident in a bath of lavender and myrrh."

"That counts," Suzie says.

"It all counts. Unless you quit counting."

"So quit counting, for a change. Stop giving grades out. Those two were up against it. Their troubles made yours look ridiculous."

Compare and contrast. Difference between. Someone to measure themselves against. Maybe that. As in: Fluffy and a skunk named Rosemary. A bear and a cat in a tree.

Maybe the cat Tuk shot out of that tree that day made Bird think of her father, of riding around with her father—spring, and everything wants to move. Her father hit a bear. The thing leapt off the bank into the road—small still, a yearling. The bear didn't move but it lived.

They were close to home and they went back and Bird's father came out with his gun. Bird didn't want to go back with him, but she thought if she didn't go back with him that something worse would happen—the bear would come at her father and he would be alone and she would be a mile away, crying.

"So I went with him. I watched him shoot the bear. I helped him drag it into the back of the car so he could take it home and skin it. A skinned bear looks like a human, they say. I never looked at it. I don't guess I ever will."

Never will. Never would. Again see him, or feel now again what he had been.

When Suzie came back with Mickey from Florida, she came back with stories to tell. He spat on his hand to shine the designer shoes of sorority girls who talked to him, and he called everybody Bird. Ignited kernels of popcorn and tossed them at women's hair.

He sent a postcard image of an antediluvian fish shot in the side with an arrow.

I am having my midnight panic again, something I'd almost forgotten. I love you completely. I daydream of you and tie you to a bridge and slowly take down your hair. I can't help you. I'm gone. Don't try to find me.

They went on and at last found See's. Tuk dragged the bag of peanuts inside and the lady at See's stood and watched him. She watched him stuff his pockets with lollipops, just as he had said he would do, and she bought his peanuts anyway, in the grip of a tender feeling. He must have looked like someone she had loved once and hoped to love again.

When Tuk had stuffed his pockets, he collected his check and walked back to the Ryder. Tuk's pockets made him walk as if he'd pissed himself or poured half a jug of milk down his pants, which he did before long to be funny. To make Doll Doll laugh and keep with him. To think she might forgive him. Forget he couldn't read, forgive him. Forget he had rented a four-room truck hoping she would sleep on a bedroll with him with the peanuts in back if the snow came, if the nights were soggy or cold. Forget the little crimson patch on his ass. The way his eyes swung loose in their sockets. Forget he was a man who had been a boy who had hidden from his mother in a pile of leaves not thinking that she might, happily, in a hurry to get to her lover, drive over her boy thinking: this is a pile of leaves. Not that boy. Not a boy who set a Have-a-Heart trap his rabbit at a clap walked into. Stuck there. Pushed out her eleven babies. Which stuck.

"Which—tell them that little story, Tuk, about the rabbits, that time, and the Have-a-Heart trap. Tell that," Doll Doll said, "or let me."

She went on.

"Eleven teensy babies. He had to drown ever one in a bucket."

"I didn't want to," Tuk said.

"Of course you didn't."

He swung the Ryder back up on the freeway, the ramp just north of the totem he had built in honor of the tumbling nugget. When he got to it again, he cut the engine.

"Hey, rider," Tuk said, "you riders," pleased with his joke, "got a beer?"

They passed another Pabst between them. "All's we need now is tapato chips," Tuk said.

"And dip," Doll Doll said. "And chocolates. I could kill for a cherry in those chocolate balls with that milky stuff that squeams out."

From under her bubbly bodysuit, she pulled out a box she had stolen from See's. She clambered over the bench seat to sit on Mickey's lap. Touched her finger to his mouth.

"That's pretty," she said, and swung the near door open.

A crow cawed in a tree. It didn't sound right.

It sounded too much like a human trying to sound like a crow.

"Here's to a first and a last." Tuk drank. "First time we saw the baby kick."

"First toothache," Bird said.

And Mickey: "Next to last can of beer."

"First time I ever tried Goobers," Doll Doll said. "I truly had no idea."

She slid out and left the door open.

She stood in the cold in her culotte and bent over the totem and said, "That's my first time I ever could feel it. Boy-oh-god that was weird."

"Last peanuts!" Tuk belted it out like a carny.

"Last bag of Sunshine peanuts! Best little nut you'll ever know."

They went on. The snow quit and night came on. Cars got off the freeway and left it to the trucks, to the all-night drivers jangly from milkshakes and days of dipping snuff.

Mickey drove for a time to let Tuk sleep slumped against the door with a pup in each hand, with Bird shoved up against him.

Tuk smelled of asparagus, cooked too long. Of age, the corridors of a nursing home, a mash of simmered prunes. He smelled of the milk he had poured down his pants.

Or that's me I'm smelling, Bird thought—smear of seed, her hair unwashed, the honey of her leaking gum. She probed her tooth with her tongue—nasty, tasty—nectar, brine. Hyacinths in an airtight room, the softened stalk succumbing.

They were out from under the snow now and the sky was the velvety purple it gets and spread all around with stars. The mountains looked like cutouts of mountains, treeless and white, tacked down on the dark plateau. Through the sage the humped Brahma wandered with cactus spines poked into their muzzles.

They saw a girl with one shoe in an organdy dress, a string of donkeys hitched to a barbed wire fence, a tinker's lonesome wagon tricked out with ribbons and cans. The first of the Sangre de Cristo's, they saw—blue in the moon, a blanked-out face the blood of Christ ran down.

Scarcely a car passed. A low rider came at them in their lane with the headlights popped off. Mickey gunned it. They could see him clear. Big yellow truck in the moonlight.

"Go easy," Tuk said, and was asleep again.

"Don't sleep," Mickey said. "I need you."

The moon sailed high and white overhead and the pale shaft of Mickey's cock appeared again in his hand.

Kill me off, Bird thought, *before I lose him.*

Drive a spike into my head.

She had her shirt off, two buttons popped, before they reached the flung shadow of a boulder Bird flattened her hands against. Mickey's breath was fast and raspy and seemed to come not from him but from the boulders strewn, from strandings of trinket and bone. Old stomping ground, detritus of fickle gods. A patch of snow like melted nickels.

Mickey toppled his boots for Bird to stand on, on the clothes heaped at their feet. Now he was in her, disappearing, shade to shade, his cock like a bull's in the shadow they cast. Bird slickened with blood she was losing still; on her breasts, hieroglyphs of his hands. Mineral seep. Her feet were pewter; a beetle wandered in the swales of her tendons, daubing methodically at the spatter of her blood. A speckled wing, iridescent. Nothing more moved but Mickey, Bird—a shadow fused, a Gorgon's head.

"It hurts, it hurts."

"Shut up, Bird."

A cloudshadow passed across them and for an instant even the supple became stone and what quivered held its tongue. The beetle raised a leg in the air.

Yes. *Be still. Be still.*

Their time was passing.

A star sputtered out. Now the moon appeared and Mickey began again, the panic of stillness gone.

The beetle went about its evening, its antenna bent inquiringly, varnished in the light of the moon. Moon on the face of the mountain. They saw no one but someone was near.

"Don't stop," Bird said. "It doesn't matter. Please."

A coyote, a bird. Something.

It was dark and looking on.

Mickey muttered, "Jesus, fucking jesus."

No word now, something older—ragged, collapsing— hymn of the lesser animals, gibberish of the gods.

Everybody looked to be sleeping when Bird and Mickey got back to the truck.

Doll Doll had eaten all but the last four rounds off the string of her candy necklace; these lay like bright stones against her throat. Mickey lifted her head and laid it in his lap and started the truck and drove on. He had blood on his cheek Bird wiped clean for him, everything in her still thrumming.

Doll Doll hummed along to the radio. Mickey turned the dial to country. Doll Doll was sleeping but the words came to her. He made a sound like a telephone and Doll Doll said, "Ring ring ring."

She howled with the coyotes. Cheered on the Lakers. He tried opera and she reached for that.

"She'll do that," Tuk said, waking now. "It's peculiar. When I found her in Waxahatchie asleep on the floor of the station, she was balled up and sucking her thumb. She sucks her thumb yet. She will in a minute. She might say something in Sioux."

The three of them watched Doll Doll sleep, her face shown in full to the moon.

"She's pretty," Tuk said. "She's just a kid, really. I got to care for her. I don't quite know as I can. I cannot read nor write, this is true. I fought fires for a time but I quit that. I got burned over twice and stopped—in these mountains here once and on the prairie. I laid down where a homesteader proved up, in a ditch he had dug with a shovel when there were bison all over this country yet, before the railroad and Little Big Horn, when Custer cut his hair and they killed him. I can't do that anymore. I'm past it. You got to be quick and young."

Tuk held his hands open to the moonlight like a map he could not decipher. He dropped them to his lap and went on.

"I fought a grass fire in old Montana once. Hope not to see such a thing again. You don't know what lives in the short grass until you set fire to it. It's creepy with snakes and beetles, your birds that nest up on the ground. Killdeer, curlew, partridge. Fox denned up and badger, coyotes and pronghorn fawns. You can't see it when you're just moving through. Everybody wants to move through. Boy wants to fight fire so he starts one in a gully thinking he won't get caught. Dumb. Fire moves. You can't contain it. You got a whirlybird and a bucket and it's like spitting into a storm. Pretty soon the blaze jumps out on the prairie.

"You don't want to live to see prairie fire, friends, in a big wind, on the move. Shit, the wind. I grew up in wind. It gets in you.

"This little girl got in me, it took a heartbeat. I am not a free man. I gave it up to her, I cannot help that, in the Waxahatchie station. I didn't have to go in there. I can't remember why I did. I don't question it. Things have a way of working—for the better, for the worse, you can't say. I can say I never will shake her. There's no helping what takes hold. She was burned. Her whole back's burned up, that arm how you see. It seems peculiar but I tell you it isn't. I carried her home. Of course I did. She was burned up. If she hadn't of been burned up, I'd of left her right where she was.

"The wind changes. What was at your back is coming at you again. You can't say. You can't say where misfortune is going, my friends. You seem to suffer. Could be the best thing that ever did happen, whatever happened to you. You get scared. You can't think but you still have to choose. You dig in. You are out there with the hoppers and the antelope, friends, and the antelope can run. You're just pokey. You talk to Jesus. You talk to whoever you can. God above. Your dead mama. The wind sounds like a jet coming at you, neverlanding. Purgatory plain and true. Every hopper alive is burning. The horse patties are burning. The wind picks them up and sails them off and wherever all it drops them, fire starts up there too. Fire everywhere and the flames knocked flat like the land is a sea set to burn-ing. Knocks it all down, the wind. You lean into it. You crawl. You talk to that old homesteader who hacked out his ditches with a shovel. Proved up.

"*What are you proving now, brother? What can you stand to believe in, brother, with flames licking inside your ears?*

"I lay down in that ditch and got little. Prayed to God, prayed to Mama. *You two shuffle me out of this and I will never come back again.* I am good to my word. I am honest. I felt the weight of God's hand on my back where I lay and it was a blazing hell."

Tuk seemed to wear out and slump away and stoke himself up again. He reached across Bird and twiddled the last stones on Doll Doll's candy necklace.

"I tried living someplace else," he said. "Bluegrass country, horse country, it was pretty for a time. Was a boy there I made friends with. I worked with his pop breaking rough stock, colts fresh in off the meadows. Good people. I fairly liked it. The days were hazy. It's wet country. The dew soaks your britches to the knees every night and come again come day.

"A day came there was a blaze set to burning in the barn—some thug from a rival farm. It's a fact: there is nothing a human won't do. I got my lead rope. You can't handle but one head at a time. It is no choice you want to make but you choose. There was a colt they were buffing for the Derby in the blaze but I went for the mare I liked. I liked her for she was gentle. She had a clear kind eye. I tied my shirt across her eyes and led her out. She was a boy's. That boy when he saw the barn go up came hellbent down the road. I brought his mare out to him. I wisht I'd quit there. I wisht I'd thought to tell him—a horse will run back to it. Of a fright. I turned away back to the barn to see could I get another one out. I maybe could of. I wisht I hadn't. I never can see much ahead of myself to think into what will be.

"That boy was small and he could not hold her. The mare pulled back and broke free. Here she came. She cut hard around me. It's the nature of things, it's her nature. She runs back. Nothing tells her better than to run like hell to exactly what she knows. Run to home. Run to the rest of them burning."

"That poor boy," Bird said, and laid her hand on Tuk's arm.

"That boy tried to run in after. I am fast enough I caught him and when I caught him, he kicked and scratched at me and beat me on my head. Just a kid. I held onto him. He was hateful, he never could help it. He just hated me, how he had to. He swore he always would."

Tuk pushed his hat down against his forehead. He looked crumpled, thrown against the seat. He let a pup gnaw at his knuckles. Wolfie tore a hole in his shirtsleeve and two tiny teeth popped out. These Tuk snapped into a pocket of his shirt to give to Doll Doll when she waked.

"At times I think of that boy. He'd be a man now. I'd like to write him but I never did learn. That mare spoke to him. I'd say I saw that. He had to hate me, I'd say, there's no shame in it. That mare was yours, boy. You took and kept her. You were a good boy. I never could."

"Well it's a story," Suzie says. "Nothing wrong with it. It's something to pass the time."

Kill the time, Bird thinks. *That's what she's saying.*

"Mama," her boy says, "Mama, I wish I could buy you a time machine, Mama. Then when you get really old, we can go back to when we were babies. Or we can go back just to now."

"What's the best thing of your day?" Bird asked him, asks him nightly, before she gets up and shuts the door.

He breathed into her face and whispered, "Being right here."

"You wish," Suzie says.

"Don't be cranky."

"How old would she be," Suzie wonders, "the girl you and Mickey didn't have?"

"I haven't done the math," Bird lies.

"You have too."

Fourteen. Feather of a hawk. Her mother's scarf wound into her hair.

"Have you?"

"Done what?"

"Done the math, Suzie Q."

"On your dead baby, or mine?"

Suzie says, "When the black widow female is ready to mate, she vibrates her web. The male advances. He winds her in silk. The positions they take are extravagant. Great contortions. Only rarely does he get away. Commonly she devours him, a widow by choice and practice. That's me. I sink my teeth in slowly and suck them entirely dry."

"I think you flatter yourself," Bird says.

"He hasn't come back."

"Your poet."

"Him."

"He'll be back," Bird says. "You need to tie him up."

"Nail him to the cross."

"What more?"

"The exploding harpoon leaves a hole in a whale big enough for a man to lie down in."

"Nice."

"And the octopus—"

"Is it gruesome, Suzie?"

"It's nature. Nature's a maniac, too."

"Tell me later, okay? The baby—"

"The male sends out a severed tentacle loaded with his seed. She tucks it away. Guards it. Waits. For death, for life, all of it. She dies days after her babies are born, dozens of them, maybe hundreds. They eat what's left of her. Simple need. Last act. It was like that, fucking Mickey. Last act every time. Like you would die from it. It would kill you."

"And it wouldn't matter," Bird says.

"It wouldn't matter."

"Like an emergency."

"Repeated."

"One more last time."

You're like God used to be. Not God, I mean, but the thing in me that listens to me think and what I say. You're all through me, Bird. I'm all you now. Cunt and mouth and eyes.

They rode on. Two-lane road through the desert, the moon tossing shadows around. They went along for a time with the headlights off until Tuk found what he was looking for, a neon sign flashing above the sagebrush: SLEEP SLEEP SLEEP.

They parked a ways off, left the pups and went in.

Tuk had a key to a room he carried. They found the room vacant. Smell of smoke. Two hard narrow beds. They turned the heat on high and the TV soft and fell away into bed.

Slept. Having slept, Tuk waked and waked Doll Doll. Mama-talked his Doll Doll. And went and went and went.

Tuk slept in his red bandanna, in his boxers and floppy socks. He waked and paced and his socks threw sparks and Doll Doll lay sucking her thumb.

Come morning, Doll Doll pulled his boxers down for him and rolled deodorant over his balls. Squeezed a seepy imperfection from his scrotum.

Tuk pulled a fresh shirt over his head.

Big Boys Hold It, the shirt read. But nobody read it to him.

They fluffed the pillows and smoothed out the sheets. Folded the little triangle back into the tail of the toilet paper. Hustled quietly out.

They found the Ryder locked with the keys inside. The pups had torn up the bench seat and squirmed in among the hillocks and tufts under the vinyl flap to keep warm. They yipped and lunged at the windows, the windows smeared and fogged.

The air smelled of dust and sagebrush and the sign was still flashing: SLEEP. The S flickered out while they watched it. The sky paled above the eastern reef where the sun would soon be up. Patches of snow were shored up where sagebrush grew and there the dust lay flattened and dark.

Everybody quiet but the birds.

Hear the birds.

Tuk found a rock, round a little and big enough, and Doll Doll made faces in the far window to lure the pups to a safer side. The rock bounced off the glass and struck Tuk in the teeth.

Doll Doll found a bigger rock and handed this one to Mickey.

"Throw it hard," Doll Doll said, and Mickey did, and the quiet of morning was over.

Tuk reached in and pulled the door open and the pups came tumbling out. They shot off across the parking lot and scratched at the motel doors.

Doll Doll started out after them—too late, too slow, Tuk had her. He picked her off her feet and heaved her into the truck. She was swinging at his face and spitting, calling the puppies' names.

"Make your move," Tuk said.

At first they didn't.

But then Mickey and Bird got in.

They drove an hour watching the sideview for whoever might come up behind. Nobody came. Doll Doll pouted and said not a word. She shivered: it was cold in the truck with the window out. They were thrashing each other with their hair.

Crows pecked at roadkill, too smart to be hit, the wiseacre scolds of the roadside. A tree way off. A glum little clump of boulders.

"The day will warm and that window won't count. You ought to look," Tuk said, "no matter."

Doll Doll dropped her face into her bodysuit and covered her ears with her hands.

"Lookit here, lookit this country," he said, and pulled her up by her hair to see.

Shadows slid over the desert, over rock and sage and cactus, the bones of the Devonian, ash of the old caldera blown some millions of years ago.

"How it lies, lookit. You ought to. The hogbacks and the coulees, the butte-tops flat as the sea. Don't tell me. Try to make it all all over again. Try to make it from scratch, the first speck of it, from rock and dark and water. Nothing was. Yet things took hold and lived. I'm not a preacher or a church dog either. Junkyard dog, most like it. But my place and my prayers are here. Bit of sage and all the many ways of the grasses. You get up on a reef and look over. Look out. You pick up a stone and throw it. It makes a little *tink* that travels, light on the wind, here to Texas. It's not the onliest thing I have come to that speaks to the lonesomeness in me. Still it speaks. Here was the first I heard it."

A big wind came up and shook them. A red tail swooped through the power lines and hooked a lizard in its talons. Banked away.

It seemed the end of something.

"I think we'll go," Mickey announced. "Stretch our legs some. I like everything you said."

They got their Glad bags out and thanked Tuk and Doll Doll, and stood in the road in the day warming up. The yellow truck got small and smaller yet on the straight road going and was gone.

They walked. Talked a little, walking.

Where to go. What to do.

They could walk on back and get Wolfie. They would have to name him again. Name him Tuk—naw. Waxahatchie. Squirt.

They walked to the bus terminal in Santa Fe. It took the day and then some. It was sunny and they walked without shoes, keeping the mountains to the east until they gave out and what was left was unbroken plateau.

Oaxaca, they talked of, Lubbock.

The drifting Sahara, the Nile.

Cuernavaca, the great Sonora.

Punta Arenas, Ushuaia, the reach of the knowable world.

Somehow they didn't have it in them. In the end they took a bus out of Santa Fe that went north again through Cimarron, east, east until the streets grew narrow again and the buildings were closing in. They took the turn for home. They called it home without even thinking. They went back to what they knew.

We came home, Bird wrote to her mother. *It's not much.*

Something could have changed but it didn't.

I can't say.

We found a place for ourselves. Not the Taj Mahal but the heat works and but for one minor riot and gunshots at night, it is quiet. The train passes and rattles the windows and our dishes stacked together in the cupboards. That, too. And cops thrash the weeds with their billy sticks. We throw bottles against the walls for the fuck of it. That, too. And Mickey doesn't touch me.

I had my tooth pulled.

He broke his hand slugging the wall.

He doesn't touch me.

We make our trips to the hospital—he mixes this with that. Breaks his hand against the wall. Opens his wrist in the tub.

I thought you kept people safe by watching, Mother.

I watch Mickey. I try to.

Something I learned from you.

Winter eased up and set back in. The apartment was built above a garage and mornings, half asleep, they heard the landlord start up his car and go. The train passed. Bird hardly went out of their bedroom. Scarcely ate. Mickey had a doctor named Dr. Money they never paid a nickel to.

Mickey picked up jobs and quit them or didn't bother to show up at all. He left for work and never reached there and his boss called to ask where he was. Bird had no idea.

And the man said, "Sweetpea, I bet you do."

Mickey lashed himself by his ankles to the doorway of their room.

"I didn't want you to find me gone," he said.

Else he went off.

Sometimes she found him. He was in a coffee shop eating plantains. He was sitting on the steps of the garage.

Else hours went by she couldn't find him and the bars emptied and filled again and beetles went about on their snelled feet through the slick tubes of Bird's head.

He wrote: *It is morning and I miss you. I loved you completely. You will never be loved better—how it pleases me to think this. Don't be afraid, Bird. I feel like setting fire to our bed, Bird, to everything you have worn with me. Everything you have taken off for me. Your letters, your shoes.*

Where are you?

Where have you been?

Please tell me I've got it all wrong, Bird. Songbird. I need you. Stay.

There were nights Bird went home when dark closed in and nights she went on walking. Past the hospital, past the morgue. She called every ER in the city but she never could call the morgue. Still she ran the loop in her head. Bird watched herself draw the sheet back; his eyes were open as when he slept. She stood in the humming refrigerated green and read the tag they had tied to his toe. It was a number and the number kept changing. It was a name Bird never had given him. Man Afraid. Looks at the Stars.

Never to walk in sunshine again.

He walks in *his sleep. I try to follow.*

He still sleeps with his eyes open, Mother. But now I know to close them like the hinged eyes of a doll.

I need an animal, Bird sometimes thought, something to sing to and feed. Something quiet and soft that would be hard to kill but that wasn't meant to live too long. A rabbit. No. A tiny donkey. A monkey to ride around on her head. Too smart, she thought. Something softer. Pocket lemur. Lamb.

Bird came back one night to find her paintings slashed—the painting of a smoking volcano, the painting of a silver-lined cloud.

So he was home.

No. No Mickey.

He had come home and gone out again.

Maybe he hasn't gone far, Bird thought, or maybe he is in here hiding?

So she looked for him and, looking, found the rest of what he had destroyed. All the many things he had made for her—the little clay pot she kept her earrings in, the earrings of salvaged tin. The box he made for her to keep her letters in, he had beaten apart with a hammer. Bird began to read the letters and stopped.

She called Suzie and Suzie was elsewhere.

Bird smashed a bottle against the wall and somebody outside shouted, "The fuck?"

It wasn't Mickey.

Mickey could never have done this.

Mickey was sinking in his ragtop through the cold black waters of the tidal strait, the sweet and the salt mixing, the tide tugging at his hair. He was at the bar eating soup and sobering up, preparing an explanation. Composing an apology, getting ready to begin again.

Bird rode out on her bicycle to look for him again, slush on the streets, *shh shh,* the wheel still out of true. She rode past a boy walking in the street and he reached out and yanked her hair. Hauled her over, felled her.

He'd been burned. He stood above her a minute with his boot on her cheek swinging his scarred hands. His teeth were tiny and soft and blue. He kept dragging his tongue across them. He will eat me if I move, Bird thought, and so she lay in the street in the spatter of glass until he walked off whistling. He whistled Dixie, as her mother had—loud and clear and true.

And Mickey came home and loved her. She had glass in her elbow and her buttons were off and he kissed her everyplace slowly as though he would not ever see her again.

"He's like a drug they quit making. It's tedious. You need to want something else."

"I do," Bird insists.

"He threw your clothes out, sugar. He rode your bicycle into the river. That's love? Think. He swung into you with a Buick. That's love? It might be love but it won't help you live."

"That Buick," Bird reminds Suzie, "is the one you went south with him in. It never smelled right. It smelled like other people. When he came back, it smelled like you."

"Bird," Suzie says.

"That's love, I guess. You said nothing. You rode the bus back. 'Where have you been?' I asked. You said nothing."

"That was ages ago," Suzie insists.

"Ages, yes. The cretaceous. The mammal has scarcely appeared. And time heals, we all know that. Better yet, it erases. Never happened! Wiped out! Off the record, free and clear. I'm not so good at it. Forgive me."

"You're forgiven," Suzie says.

"Fuck you."

Bird had scratched Mickey's name in the windshield and hers with the ruby her mother had given her.

Given her. Forgiven her.

For the C days, the D days, Bird hoped to be forgiven.

For pinworms, forgive me.

For the pup tumbling down the stairs.

For watching Mickey and not watching Mickey and the names she never called him by. By her own name he gave her, mistaken.

For opening his eyes while he slept: *I am right here.*

Bird draws a finger down the flat of the baby's foot and her toes bunch up. Old monkey brain. The callous on her lip is like mica, bright and chipped away. Bird needs to eat, pull on a fresh pair of panties. Meet what remains of the day.

Back by the swamp is a grave mound Bird promised to neaten and keep. It still needs a cross to say *Sherderd.* Her boy had named his pup Sherderd. They went down a list of names to consider: Squirt, Bump, John. Ice Cream Fucker was another, but you couldn't call a puppy that.

Bird had left the pup at the top of the stairs, the school bus flying down the hill. Her boy bounded into the house ahead of her.

"First death," Suzie said.

Thank you, Suzie.

"The rest will be repetitions, sugar. *One more last time.*"

Bird remembered a story Tuk had told them about throwing a ball to a dog. Awful little story he had to live with. Tuk threw the ball. The dog caught it, tumbled over a near cliff and died.

"Good thing it happened a long time ago," Doll Doll said.

C days, D minus days, of course everybody had them.

The pup was heaped at the foot of the stairs. Her boy picked it up. The head swung free, the neck bone snapped.

"Mama? You will get old and bigger next and next you will go back down," he said. "I will be big as Papa. And you will be my baby. You will be just small, like this. I will carry you all around like this, like a baby, holding you tight in my hands."

"*In my hands?*" Suzie said. "Oh, sugar."

Here her breath caught.

"He could fall off the bed and keep sleeping," Suzie said, "all the long afternoon."

"Your poet?" Bird wondered.

"Our Mickey. Mine. And hers and hers and hers."

We lost our little baby like you did. But we got Wolfie back. Also Snowball.

I am writing this myself which remember I could not used to do. Doll Doll is the one what's teaching me.

Pretty lucky.

Happy trails from Tuk and Doll Doll. You remember us now, dont you?

Bird left the letter under Mickey's coffee cup for him to come home and find. He was quiet when he came home. He led her quietly to their unmade bed.

He hooked his feet in his boots beside the basket of her ribs. Rolled his knees against her arms into the sockets. Brought a pillow down over her face.

You wait so long for something to happen to you and still you are surprised when it does.

Bird took a sip of breath and waited.

Her shoulders fell apart, bone from bone. She lay quiet, holding the sip of breath she had taken.

She saw her mother at the end of her kite string and her bed from when she was a girl.

Daffodils past the window.

Blackbirds in a cottonwood tree.

It was all getting small and smaller, the marvelous knot of what she had lived and seen.

I wanted to die so I let him, Mother.

I was wrong. I wanted to live.

By morning he had gone off with Suzie.

By morning Bird had taken her clothes off for Doctor Said So to see.

He slept with *his eyes partly open, Mother. I drew the pillow out from under his head. So to close them. So that I might sleep beside him. So to wake should he wake so to follow. Should he walk out on the street, I followed him. He walked sleeping. He walked in circuits as he slept and snapped his fingers and in minutes returned to home.*

Home.

I can't see you, Mother.

I tried to leave him. I tried to quit.

I tried to love somebody else. I never could at first. I was waiting for Mickey.

I waited a time and then quit.

I quit other things I can't name quite. Quit climbing the Brooklyn Bridge. Quit junk, quit worrying he would leave me, quit worrying he would come back again.

I wrote letters to you you stopped answering. I couldn't hear you. I couldn't see you anymore.

I thought to drop off the bridge how the poets did but it seemed altogether too dumb.

Dumb bunny. Name of Hoppy.

Name of Bird, name of Bean, both and either.
I kept the names Mickey gave me.
I called him Mickey.
I don't know why. I never called him anything more.

Little Whale, White Moon.

She calls her Lollipop. Little Chicken and Wants a Lot.

Shoofly.

Sunshine.

Sprocket.

Small Fry. Wingnut. Chief.

Buckaroo.

Speed Racer.

Snowball. Noodle. Knucklehead.

Dude-a-reno. Dude.

I don't think *he meant to kill me, Mother. I just think he didn't know.*

Bird wrote: *Something is growing against the roof of my mouth, Mother. It's like cobwebs. It frays. It tastes like nothing. I roll it up with my tongue.*

I feel drugged, dragged. Wasted, Mother.

I hardly know myself.

I can't see your face. I try to see your face and my face appears.

I can't help that. I can't see through.

To get out to the street they had to go through two gates the landlord kept locked from outside. The gates were tin and corrugate and they swung out into the street. There was a padlock on the street side and a darkly oiled chain. There was a hole in each gate you had to reach through as big as a piece of paper. You reached blindly and fumbled through it. You couldn't see to the other side.

When Suzie rode the bus back from Florida, she stood in the sleet on the street side. Let her stand there, Bird thought. Explaining. She was cold. She could have said it on the phone if Bird had let her.

"Let me in," Suzie said. "It meant nothing."

Bird wanted to stand in the dark and cold with the gate swung shut between them.

"Show me your face," Bird said.

Suzie needed a coat for the cold. She was sick and she had no money.

"Show me your face," Bird said.

Suzie kneeled in the street. She pressed her face to the hole in the gate and every word Bird had thought to say to Suzie and the things she had thought to do to Suzie flared and burned away in her head. Nothing moved her. Bird turned away and went up the stairs. She came down with a coat her mother had worn and passed it through the gate to Suzie. The lining caught and tore on the gate and hung in the sleet like a wing. Bird remembered her mother in it and how the fur of the collar felt on her face and when she slid her hand through the arm of the coat how smooth it always felt like persimmon and lovely to touch and cool.

And the days passed.

And the days were weeks and the months passed.

And a day came Bird reached her hands through the gate to open the lock to find food. She fumbled with the lock. He took hold of her hands and pulled her to him from the street side where he stood. He said nothing. Her face was pressed against the gate.

At last she whispered, "Mickey, you came home."

I thought if I told him a story.

I told him about my father, I don't know why, he flew a Cessna, I made it up as I went along.

"I was a girl," I said. "I was a girl let to go with her father out in the sunshine to shoot an elephant."

I said, "It took a long time falling. It had a small bright eye."

Mickey kept quiet. He had something hard he was jabbing at me between the gates where the gates swung together.

I said, "It breaks its bones falling."

I said, "It has a small bright eye."

It was a fork maybe or a stick he had found or the key I had reached through the gate with to feel for the lock to *unlock it. It was sharp and I thought it would cut me. He drew it hard up the front of me as if to open me up to my chin.*

I said, "They come at it with a torch. Up the ass end with a torch. I don't know is it dead or living then—when they come at it with a torch. If they wait, I don't know, to get the tusks free, to burn the body out to get the tusks free, something to show for it, to make trinkets with, a pretty chess set, to make baubles with to bring home."

He held me so my face was against the gate and the metal was smooth and cold. The day was cold, I remember, and graying and we stood a long time without speaking before he let my hands go and walked away.

I went back to the apartment and undressed myself. He had not cut me, not really. He had left light bleeding marks. I deepened these with a knife I found in the kitchen among the others. I didn't know did I hope to survive him, to suffer with him, to die. To ruin ourselves together. Live to be together. I put the knife back. I can't say.

I took a few small things he had made for me that he hadn't found to destroy. I took the small bone with tooth marks in it that he had brought to me from the mountains.

We had a window I let myself out through. I followed the tracks out. I heard sirens I had heard every day for months.

I followed the tracks out. The tracks ran out through sumac, through the dry and stalky weeds where killers and rapists and pickpockets in seasons of growth squat to hide. We saw them fleeing down the tracks from our window. We saw cops thrash the weeds with their billy sticks, shouting to flush them out.

It was spring and there were places to hide now. The leaves were bright and new. Somebody walked behind me. Someone shouted in the street above my head. A bottle dropped over the high wall and bounced at my feet without breaking.

I made myself small when the train came. I felt the heat of the train and how the ground shook and in the windows as they passed I saw him see me—the man who would come for me. He would swing down over the high wall the tracks ran shining between—one pair of tracks beside the other as if to meet in a point at a distance. I saw myself twisted beneath the wheels of the train—how ugly I was and how beaten. He would wad a rag in my mouth not to hear me.

I called up. A child who was playing came to look at me. A few of his friends came to look at me and they tied one bedsheet to another as in a movie to help me up. They got me up and over the wall and I stood in their street and let them look at me. They didn't want to talk to me. They had hoped for somebody else. Someone oozing, something blue. I got to laughing. They were disgusted with me. I got to where I couldn't quit laughing and I laughed until the last boy turned from me, trailing a sheet, and walked away.

Months later I set out to look for him. I walked out of our place not knowing where I meant to go. I had money for a bus and a toothbrush, little more.

I had a street name; I knew his car. I rode the bus days

south eating peanuts, thinking of what to say. The houses brightened—washed to pink, washed to green.

His Buick was in the street, a window smashed. I sat in it and held the wheel. I pulled on his hat he had left on the seat. The street was quiet, he walked up the middle, mouthing the words, "Go home."

But for the one time he came to me, that was the last time I saw him.

"He came to me in a dream," I told Suzie.

But it wasn't a dream. It was true.

I was in the hospital after my boy was born.

Mickey appeared in the doorway. He said nothing. I told no one, but I wanted to tell someone. I told Suzie.

I said, "He came to me in a dream. He wore a velvet robe."

He brought handfuls in his pockets of petals fallen from apple trees. I was drugged still and dopey. He made a trail between us with petals he dropped and he walked on the petals to reach me. He drew the sheet back. They had cut me open. The wind had torn up his hair.

"I loved you once," he said, and let the sheet fall back, "but then a day came. It seemed as nothing, everything we had."

We had had a baby and lost her. It was common, it wasn't uncommon. People came back from it; they endured. Suffered and endured and got on with it, that was the idea.

But how was it we had lost her? Mickey wanted to know.

Did she die of us not wanting her, of something he had said, of the cold?

We had a drawer for a bed, an old dog-hairy blanket.

Not much. More than some. Plenty.

Was it the junk we snorted?

Was it just that we wanted to keep on—talking how we did and digging into ourselves and climbing up the struts of the bridge in the wind—to wonder how not to do it: live: not to live: not to live long enough to lose each other and so to die in the old way, happy?

We were happy. Was that so hard to stand?

Was can't last *what made it bearable or* can?

Can last? Can? Can have? Could?

What if that?

What if they had been careful and ready to want what would be—a life, another, a baby, his, little Caroline, little Caroline, what if Bird had—he was twisting her hair around the palm of his hand—and what if he had wanted her, too?

Bird hears a little sound like choking.

It comes out "Ng."

"What is it?" Bird says. "What happened?"

"I can't."

"It's your poet."

"No."

"He hurt you."

"No."

"You're evicted."

"Bird."

"You're dying. You talked to the doctor."

"No. No."

"It's Mickey."

"Bird."

Bird waits a minute, guesses again.

"He's married," Bird says. "Or you are."

"Ng."

Suzie has to hang up and call again.

"I'm finished," she says at last.

She has had her tubes tied. Nothing is going to live in her.

"I will never give blood again."

Bird pictures Suzie in a wedding dress.

Pregnant. Infant in Arms.

The picture shrinks to nothing in her head.

She pictures Tuk and Doll Doll, a tar paper house, their pawky stream. Tuk writing to Bird in the kitchen.

Happy trails.

Bronco boys, limping. Tuk walking his girl to the street dance, rosy-cheeked from the sun. In the dirt, wild bunched-up rose.

Bird sees a road roll out.

Days of such wind you can't walk straight. Eddies of dust, a buoyant seed. How the wind there blew, it blows.

Hang your head over, Bird sings to the baby. *Hear the wind, hear the wind blow.*

Bird carries the baby in her bouncy seat out to sit in the last of the sun. Together they wait for the school bus.

October. The windows gilded. The luminous afternoon.

The trees look painted—the reds, the orange and yellow. Even the tamarack is going yellow, the needles twisting down. Somebody is mowing a last time. Somebody rakes. It's all fine. Beautiful, really. White houses, red weathering off the barn. Bird loves the barn—the dark mouth of it, swallows dipping through.

A blue day.

A field of seven white cows.

It feels mild, an old person's country.

The shut-in days ahead of her, the gentle closing in. Soon the trees will be picked clean and the branches will show and the nests of birds and foxes deep in the leafless woods. The trees shade out the understory. They are old, and stand together touching.

Here it comes: the bus whistling at last down the hill.

Her boy leaps from the steps. He has got his coat on over his backpack, inside out and upside down.

"Hello, my prince."

"Did you give away the baby yet?"

Bird picks him up and swings him, forgetting she can't do it.

"Hurts," she says, and goes to her knees and he climbs on her back to help her. He has his face in her hair. Bird feels the heat of him, the wild, swift heart. The straps of his golden backpack.

"You smell funny, Mama. Mama, you smell like the second time you tried to make miso soup."

"Sprocket," Bird says, "hop off."

He throws his coat to the grass and runs around. Runs to the top of the hill and rolls down it, smashing everything in his backpack until he's lying on it, looking up at her.

"I made you a picture of a cheetah."

He smoothes the paper against the grass, a cat in the grass, the crayon rubbed to a high shine where he has worked it hard for color.

He says, "Mama, I love cheetahs wicked almost as you."

Bird moves her shadow across him to keep the sun from his eyes. A fly lights on his cheek and she shoos it. The baby flutters her milky arms.

God above. Unholy love.

Bird is burning up and collapsing. She is ash and dazzled, rapt—gone to her knees in pieces in the wind of a passing world.